Oliver Optic

Lightning Express or the Rival Academies

Oliver Optic

Lightning Express or the Rival Academies

ISBN/EAN: 9783337270889

Printed in Europe, USA, Canada, Australia, Japan

Cover: Foto ©Andreas Hilbeck / pixelio.de

More available books at **www.hansebooks.com**

R. SAVIA — DEL

THE MAN ON THE RAFT. Page 140.

LAKE SHORE SERIES.

BY

OLIVER OPTIC.

LIGHTNING EXPRESS.

LEE & SHEPARD.
BOSTON.

THE LAKE SHORE SERIES.

LIGHTNING EXPRESS;

OR,

THE RIVAL ACADEMIES.

BY

OLIVER OPTIC,

AUTHOR OF "YOUNG AMERICA ABROAD," "THE ARMY AND NAVY STORIES,"
"THE WOODVILLE STORIES," "THE BOAT-CLUB STORIES,"
"THE STARRY FLAG SERIES," ETC.

BOSTON:
LEE AND SHEPARD, PUBLISHERS.
NEW YORK:
LEE, SHEPARD AND DILLINGHAM.
1871.

TO

MY YOUNG FRIEND

JAMES DEWITT CARSON

𝔗𝔥𝔦𝔰 𝔅𝔬𝔬𝔨

IS AFFECTIONATELY DEDICATED.

THE LAKE SHORE SERIES.

1. *THROUGH BY DAYLIGHT;* or, The Young Engineer of the Lake Shore Railroad.

2. *LIGHTNING EXPRESS;* or, The Rival Academies.

3. *ON TIME;* or, The Young Captain of the Ucayga Steamer.

4. *SWITCH OFF;* or, The War of the Students.

5. *BRAKE UP;* or, The Young Peacemakers.

6. *BEAR AND FORBEAR;* or, The Young Skipper of Lake Ucayga.

PREFACE.

LIGHTNING EXPRESS is the second volume of the LAKE SHORE SERIES, and has been published in Oliver Optic's Magazine, Our Boys and Girls. The story, like its predecessor, relates to the Lake Shore Railroad, though the war between the rival academies occupies a considerable portion of the book. Waddie Wimpleton and Tommy Toppleton, as they appear in these volumes, are not strangers, in real life, to the writer; and probably all his readers are familiar with similar young gentlemen in their own spheres.

The author has endeavored to keep the moral movement of the story up to the proper standard, and is not afraid that any reasonable young man will like either Tommy or Waddie well enough to imitate their conduct, while he is satisfied that all will be pleased with the moral heroism of Wolf Penniman, and will indorse his views of Christian duty.

HARRISON SQUARE, MASS.,
July 21, 1869.

CONTENTS.

CHAPTER I.
PAGE

A Stockholders' Meeting. 11

CHAPTER II.

The Stockholders in Council. 22

CHAPTER III.

The President of the Road. 34

CHAPTER IV.

Off for the Camp. 45

CHAPTER V.

A Breezy Prospect ahead. 57

CHAPTER VI.

A Mission of Peace. 69

CHAPTER VII.

Major Tommy gets mad. 81

CHAPTER VIII.

CHARGE BAYONETS! 93

CHAPTER IX.

FEATHERS AND THE ENGINEER. 104

CHAPTER X.

KEEPING THE PEACE. 116

CHAPTER XI.

AT THE HORSE SHOE. 128

CHAPTER XII.

UP THE LAKE. 139

CHAPTER XIII.

IF THINE ENEMY HUNGER. 150

CHAPTER XIV.

COLONEL WIMPLETON BIDS HIGH. 162

CHAPTER XV.

THE IMPENDING BATTLE. 174

CHAPTER XVI.

THE BATTLE OF THE HORSE SHOE. 186

CHAPTER XVII.

THE PRISONER OF WAR. 198

CHAPTER XVIII.

RESCUING A PRISONER. 210

CHAPTER XIX.

A TYRANNICAL SON. 222

CHAPTER XX.

THE LIGHTNING EXPRESS TRAIN.. 233

CHAPTER XXI.

MAKING UP TIME. 244

CHAPTER XXII.

THE NEW FIREMAN. . . . . - . . 254

CHAPTER XXIII.

THE PRESIDENT AND THE ENGINEER. 266

CHAPTER XXIV.

THE PRESIDENT HAS A FALL. 278

CHAPTER XXV.

THE PRESIDENT IN TROUBLE. 290

CHAPTER XXVI.

THE NEW STEAMER. 300

LIGHTNING EXPRESS;

OR,

THE RIVAL ACADEMIES.

CHAPTER I.

A STOCKHOLDERS' MEETING.

"ORDER, gentlemen, order!" said Mr. Tommy Toppleton, rapping his gavel on the desk before him. "While I am president of the Lake Shore Railroad, I will have order!"

Tommy was the son of his father; on this question there could be no dispute. Not only was his father a great man, but Tommy, in his own estimation, was a great man also; on this question, unfortunately, there was some dispute. Perhaps it was the young gentleman's misfortune, certainly it was not his fault, that he was the only son of a very rich father, and had been indulged until he was, so far as the circumstances would admit, a spoiled child. He had many excellent qualities; but he had come to think that among the boys he was the central figure, and that without him they were nothing, and could do nothing.

Tommy regarded other boys, even the students of the Toppleton Institute who were his equals in wealth and social position, as in some sense footballs for his capricious toes. Many of his companions did not like him, because he "put on airs," because he was overbearing and tyrannical to his inferiors, and because he always claimed the highest position and the loftiest dignity among them. When the Lake Shore Railroad Company was organized, he was elected one of the board of directors, and then by them was chosen president. He had filled this office from the beginning, and he expected always to fill it.

The company had been in operation about a year, during which time it had dealt mainly with imaginary certificates of stock, bonds, rolling stock, and other material, the object being to give the students a knowledge of railroad business. The actual building of the road had rendered the company somewhat more real; but, as all the property was in fact owned by Major Toppleton, who held the bonds of the company for its full value, it was still to the students an educational rather than a practical business enterprise. The real owner, therefore, was the real manager of the road. He told the directors what votes to pass, and they were pliant enough to obey. All the forms of electing officers, appointing the superintendent, road-master, engineers, and other officers, were punctiliously adhered to.

The capital stock of the company was two hundred thousand dollars, represented by two thousand shares of one hundred dollars each, which had been apportioned among the students of the Institute, in unequal parts. Some owned one hundred shares, others only two or three. Tommy Toppleton was the happy possessor of a quarter part of the capital stock of the concern, and threw five hundred votes, each representing a share, in a stockholders' meeting. An account was kept with each owner of

stock, and transfers from one to another were frequent. I am sorry to detract from the dignity of
the enterprise by confessing that a share, whose par
value was one hundred dollars, was frequently bar-
tered away for a pint of pea-nuts, though, as the
road, like many others, was mortgaged for its full
value, perhaps the compensation was adequate.

Two thousand mortgage bonds of one hundred
dollars each had been issued, duly signed by the
officers, and bearing interest at seven per cent. As
the company had no receipts for the first quarter
of the year, the railroad was heavily in debt, and
the students were not likely to be burdened with
any extra spending money from their dividends. I
had run the dummy during the fall and winter,
carrying passengers as far as Grass Springs; not for
the fun of it, but at regular fares — twenty cents
to Spangleport, five miles distant, fifty cents to the
Springs, thirteen miles, and between the two latter
points, thirty cents. There had been considerable
travel, enough to make a breeze with the steamboat company, though not enough to pay the interest and expenses of running.

As the students were not permitted to neglect their studies for the purpose of serving as conductors and engineers, outsiders had been employed to some extent. Major Toppleton did not regard the Lake Shore Railroad as a mere plaything. During the winter he had procured his charter, and he had expended an immense sum of money on the road since he commenced, for his ideas had enlarged as he progressed, and he intended to have a regular line to Ucayga, at the foot of the lake. In a quiet way he had bought up the stock of the steamboat company, and a report was circulated in the spring that the boats would run only between Middleport and Hitaca, at the head of the lake, when the railroad was completed. The Centreporters were filled with horror and indignation, for this scheme would leave them no means of communication with Ucayga, on the great lines of railroad, except by the way of Middleport, and would compel them to patronize the hated Lake Shore line. But this project was only rumored; it had not yet been developed.

The assembly in which Mr. Tommy Toppleton insisted that order should be preserved while he

was the president of the Lake Shore Railroad, was
the annual meeting of the stockholders, at which the
election of officers was to take place. By permission of Major Toppleton I was allowed to own five
shares in the road, though, as I was not a member
of the Institute, I was not eligible as a purchaser
of stock. But I felt an interest in the enterprise,
and an interest in the method of conducting the
business, and I had purchased my stock at a fearful depreciation from the par value. One of the
fellows, by the name of Limpenfield, had run out
of pocket money, and being sorely tempted to enjoy a feast of cream cakes, I had taken advantage
of his necessities, and bought five shares for twenty-
five cents!

The meeting threatened to be rather stormy, for
I happened to know that there were two tickets
in the field for a board of directors, on one of
which the name of Tommy Toppleton did not appear, though the canvassing had been so carefully
conducted that the person principally concerned had
no suspicion of his own unpopularity, and least of
all that the stockholders would have the audacity

to tip him out of his exalted position. But this question had not yet come to an issue. The excitement was over another matter.

"I move you that we proceed to the election of officers at once," said Barnscott.

"I move you that we adjourn to Grass Springs!" shouted Wetherstane.

"Second the motion!" added Putnam.

"Order, gentlemen! What motion do you second, Putnam?" demanded the president.

"The motion to adjourn to Grass Springs, of course."

"What do we want to adjourn to Grass Springs for?" demanded Barnscott.

"Question! Question!" called the crowd.

"There is no motion before the stockholders!" roared Tommy, hammering the desk vigorously with his gavel, for he was a model presiding officer, and would no more have served in this capacity without a gavel than he would have gone to meeting without a coat.

"Mr. President, I made a motion," said Barnscott.

"So did I," added Wetherstane.

"Neither of them is before the house. Gentlemen, you interrupt the company's business by your
disorder. I insist that the proceedings be conducted
with parliamentary propriety." Tommy had been to
the legislature with his father when the charter was
obtained, and indulged in technical phrases which
all the students did not fully comprehend.

"I move you —"

"Order!" screamed Tommy, at the top of his
lungs, and as savage as a yellow wasp.

"I move you —"

"Order!" repeated the vigorous president, indicating each of the movers by pointing at them
with his gavel. "Take your seat, Barnscott! Sit
down, Wetherstane! This business shall be done
in an orderly manner, or not at all;" and Tommy
swelled up till he was as big as the presiding
officer of the Senate of the United States.

"I thought this was a free country, and that
the stockholders of the Lake Shore Railroad had
a right to speak in the meetings," growled the irre-
pressible Barnscott.

"Sit down!" thundered Tommy.

"I have a certificate for ten shares; and that gives me the right to speak and to vote in this meeting," added the indignant Wetherstane.

"Take your seat, or I will have you put out of the hall!" yelled the president.

"I'll sell my stock to any fellow that wants it for a stick of molasses candy," continued the wrathy Barnscott. "What is the use of owning stock if you are to be muzzled like a mad dog?"

"Shall we have order, or not?" cried the president, disgusted with the irregular proceedings of the turbulent stockholders.

"Order! Order!" shouted a respectable majority of the assembly.

Tommy was evidently out of breath, and disposed to resort to disagreeable measures. The meeting was held in the chapel of the Institute, and the principal, if not the major, was within calling distance. Rather than have a lecture from either of them, the violent makers of motions subsided for a time, and permitted the president to do the lecturing. Tommy took a swallow of water from a tumbler on the desk, and then looked majestically around the room, as if to satisfy himself that no further disorder was intended, and that the turbulent ones were disposed to listen to his remarks.

"Gentlemen, order is Heaven's first law, and it must be the first law of the Lake Shore Railroad Company, especially in a meeting of its stockholders," Tommy began, and then paused, looking as solemn as an owl at noonday, to note the effect of his impressive words.

As no one objected to this proposition, Tommy took another swallow of cold water, and proceeded with his remarks.

"No business can be done while we are in confusion," he continued, with due seriousness, as he straightened back his neck. "This is a parliamentary assembly, like the legislature of the state, and we purpose to do all things in a parliamentary manner. Such bodies, met together for purposes of debate, are subject to certain well-established rules, sanctioned by usage, and governed by precedents."

"Whew!" whistled Briscoe. "I wonder what book he stole that from."

"I beg your pardon, Mr. President, but I made a motion, which was properly seconded," interrupted Wetherstane, quite mildly now. "I don't think any other business can be brought before the house till that one has been settled."

"The motion was in order, — a motion to adjourn is always in order, — but it was not properly before the stockholders. The motion does not become a question, and is not before the house, until it has been stated by the presiding officer. A motion cannot be entertained until it has been seconded; and made and seconded, it does not become a question until it has been stated by the president. One question must be disposed of before another can be entertained. Gentlemen, I insist upon order. I am now ready to hear any motion;" and Tommy, having laid down the law, intended that everybody should abide by it.

CHAPTER II.

THE STOCKHOLDERS IN COUNCIL.

MR. TOMMY TOPPLETON had reduced the riotous assembly before him to a tolerable degree of subjection. The president was obliged to embody in his own person the dignity of the Lake Shore Railroad, since those in front of him refused to be conscious of the glory of being stockholders. He was ready to hear any motion, and it was evident that he intended to keep the peace. But the boys were really excited. They had been discussing the interests of the road, and some of their projects would certainly prove to be treasonable to the house of Toppleton. It must be confessed that a great many of them could not see the difference between their own interests and those of the road; and being excited, they did not set a good example to their elders in Congress and other delibera-

A STOCKHOLDERS' MEETING. — Page 23.

tive bodies, but behaved very much like full-grown men on similar occasions.

"Mr. President," said Wetherstane, springing to his feet, as soon as it was evident that a motion was in order.

"Mr. President," called Barnscott, almost at the same instant. "I move —"

"Wetherstane has the floor," interposed the impartial presiding officer, vigorously pounding the desk with his gavel; and I must say he made noise enough to entitle him to preference as one of the gentlemanly conductors on our road, where noise seemed to be at a premium.

"What sort of way is that?" demanded Barnscott. "I have the floor."

"Wetherstane attracted my attention first, and he has the floor," replied Tommy, decidedly.

"I was up first," persisted Barnscott.

"Take your seat, sir!" roared the president; and the pine boards of which the lid of the desk was composed were in imminent danger of being fractured by his gavel.

"Mr. President, I rise to a point of order," said Lennox.

"Order, gentlemen!" roared Tommy. "I have decided that Wetherstane has the floor. If any stockholder is so disposed, he can appeal from the decision of the chair."

Under ordinary circumstances, Tommy Toppleton did not permit any appeal from the decision of the chair, and always insisted upon having his own way; but it was in the nature of a triumph for him to direct the deliberations of his fellow-students, and to introduce forms and methods of which the majority of them had never heard.

"I appeal from the decision of the chair," added Lennox.

"Points of order necessarily take precedence of all other questions," said Tommy, with the utmost dignity and self-possession.

"Ahem!" coughed a fellow in the crowd, which brought down a regular board-splitter from the gavel.

"The chair decided that Wetherstane had the floor. An appeal is taken. The question now before the house is, Shall the decision of the chair stand as the decision of the stockholders? This question is debatable, and the presiding officer may participate in the discussion. You will all see that, occupying a position where I can see all the members of the assembly, I could not very well make a mistake in regard to who spoke first. I am quite confident that Wetherstane had said 'Mr. President' before Barnscott opened his mouth."

Various opinions were expressed by individual stockholders, and they were about equally divided on the merits of the question. Each claimant for the floor had half a dozen advocates, who were confident that their man had spoken first. It was really a matter between Tommy and the stockholders, which they were likely to decide as they loved or hated the president.

"Question! Question!" called the students, when they began to be weary of the fruitless debate.

"Those in favor of sustaining the decision of the chair will manifest it by saying, 'Ay.'"

"Ay!" shouted many voices.

"Those opposed say, 'No.'"

"No!" responded the determined opponents of the president.

"It is a vote!" said Tommy, who was not quite willing to believe that one of his decisions could be reversed by a majority.

"A vote!" exclaimed Lennox. "Why, Mr. President—"

"Silence, sir! A vote cannot be debated," thundered Tommy, with awful dignity. "Any member has the right to doubt the vote, and call for a count."

"I doubt the vote, Mr. President, and call for a count," added Lennox.

"The vote is doubted," said Tommy, rapping violently to repress the noise and confusion. "Those in favor of sustaining the decision of the chair will rise and stand uncovered till counted."

"Uncovered?" demanded Briscoe. "Shall we take our things off?"

"Order!"

Tommy's friends, and those who had not backbone enough to vote against his decision, rose and were counted. I voted with this side because I really believed that Wetherstane had spoken first.

"Twenty-one," said the president, after he had

counted the affirmatives; and I noticed that his lips were compressed, as if to subdue some angry emotions which he felt at the result.

"Those opposed stand till counted."

A large majority, obtaining pluck from mere numbers, sprang to their feet.

"All up! All up!" shouted the more demonstrative of the rebels, who had doubtless been to town meetings in their day.

"Order!" screamed Tommy, more fiercely than ever; for the vote, to him, looked like factious opposition. "Eighty-six in the negative," he added, when he had completed the count.

Silence reigned in the hall then, and perhaps many of the students were appalled to think of what they had done. They had actually voted down the high and mighty Tommy Toppleton, whose word was law. The experience of the nations that deliberative bodies are not favorable to the rule of tyrants was in a fair way to be realized by the heir of the house of Toppleton. The boys watched the president, expecting an outburst of indignation and wrath at his defeat; but, happily,

the dignity of the presiding officer prevailed over
the feelings of the individual, and with a mighty
struggle he repressed his emotions. As I have had
occasion to say before, Tommy was in the main a
good fellow; he would have been a first-rate one
if he had not been spoiled by the weak indulgence
of his father and mother. He had been taught to
have his own way, and his passions were a volcano
within him, ready to break out whenever he was
thwarted. I am inclined to think this was the first
time he had ever conquered himself, and restrained
his wrath when defeated.

"The decision is in the negative," added Tommy,
with admirable self-possession for one of his tempera-
ment. "Barnscott has the floor."

"Mr. President," said the lucky claimant, "I move
that we proceed to the election of officers for the
ensuing year."

"Second the motion," added Faxon.

"It is moved and seconded that the stockholders
proceed to the election of officers," continued Tommy, who could not see why all this storm had been
created on so simple a proposition. "The question
is now before the house."

"Mr. President!" shouted Wetherstane, loud enough to have been heard on the other side of Ucayga Lake.

"Wetherstane," replied Tommy, indicating that the speaker had the floor.

"I move you that we adjourn to Grass Springs at two o'clock this afternoon," added the young gentleman, who, beyond the possibility of a doubt, had the floor now.

"Second the motion," added Putnam.

"It is moved and seconded that we adjourn to Grass Springs at two o'clock this afternoon," repeated the president, wondering what this movement meant.

"What's to be done with my motion?" demanded Barnscott. "I thought one thing had to be settled before another was brought up."

"A motion to adjourn is always in order," said the president.

"Mr. President, I rise to a point of order," interposed Skotchley, a quiet kind of fellow, who had studied deeper into parliamentary law than even Tommy Toppleton, for he had been the presiding officer of a juvenile debating society.

" State your point, Skotchley."

" I respectfully submit that the motion to adjourn is not in order, for the reason that, to entitle it to precedence, it should simply be a motion to adjourn without fixing a time."

Tommy was nonplussed. The question took him out of his depth. He had Cushing's Manual in his pocket, but it would not be dignified to consult it in the presence of the stockholders. However, he knew that Skotchley was well posted, and he deemed it prudent to follow his lead.

" The chair decides that the point is well taken, and that the motion to adjourn is not in order," said he, though probably he would not have been so pliant if he had not been opposed to the substance of the motion. " By the ruling out of this motion, Barnscott's is now in order."

" That's a pretty how d'ye do !" exclaimed Putnam.

" Order ! The motion to proceed to the choice of officers is now before the house."

" Mr. President, I move to amend the motion by the addition of the words, ' at Grass Springs at two o'clock this afternoon,' " said Wetherstane.

"Second the motion," added Putnam, who was evidently "in the ring," for he seconded only the Grass Springs motions.

Tommy stated the amendment, and there was a silence of a minute or two, for a wonder. Then Barnscott did not see why the amendment had been brought forward, and wanted to know what Grass Springs had to do with election of officers. He evidently was not "in the ring." He should vote against the amendment, and he hoped all the rest of the stockholders would do the same.

"Mr. President," said Briscoe, who had more pluck than most of his companions, "who ever heard of the stockholders of a railroad holding a meeting for the election of officers right in the place where they do their business? It is contrary to custom, and I protest against any innovations. They always have a free train, and take the stockholders to a place where there is a good hotel. After they have voted, they have a first-rate supper at the expense of the corporation. If they don't always do it, they always ought to do it. I am in favor of having this meeting at the hotel in

Grass Springs, and, after the business is done, of eating as good a supper as the landlord can get up for us."

"Question! Question!" shouted the stockholders, who seemed to be unanimously in favor of following the precedent.

Barnscott made a speech in favor of an immediate election. He did not believe stockholders usually had a dinner; but, as he continued his remarks rather longer than prudence justified, he was interrupted by calls for the question.

"Are you ready for the question?" said Tommy, who did not know what to make of the remarkable proceedings of the company. "You can vote what you please, fellows; but carrying out the vote is quite another thing. You can vote that Lake Ucayga dry up if you like, but it won't dry up."

"Dry up!" shouted some of the ruder ones. "Question!"

"Those in favor of amending the motion will say 'Ay,'" added the president.

The motion was carried by a majority of three to one. The original motion was then passed by a vote of the same ratio. Briscoe then moved that the directors be instructed to make the arrangements for the meeting and the dinner in the afternoon, which was also carried. The meeting then adjourned; but it was clear enough to Tommy Toppleton that the stockholders were taking things into their own hands, and that his father would have something to say in regard to the astounding vote.

3

CHAPTER III.

THE PRESIDENT OF THE ROAD.

"WHAT does all this mean, Wolf?" said Mr. Tommy Toppleton to me, after the stockholders' meeting had adjourned.

"What does it mean?" I repeated, moved by the condescension of the high and mighty scion of the house of Toppleton in addressing me, and, in some sense, making a confidant and adviser of me.

Probably he came to me because he was rather confused in regard to the identity of his friends. As president of the Lake Shore Railroad, he had rendered a decision from which the stockholders had appealed, and he had been beaten by a vote of four to one. He was vexed and mortified at the result, and was disposed to regard it as a personal insult. He had always had his own way, and could see no reason why he should not always have it. In the excitement of building the road, the students had regarded him as the representative of his father, who was doing an immensely great thing to add to the popularity of the Toppleton Institute; and his offensive manner, his domineering, haughty, and even tyrannical conduct, had hardly been noticed. But, after the road had lost its novelty, the lordly demeanor of the little magnate was not relished, and he was beginning to feel the effects of his conduct.

I did not like to tell Tommy even as much of the real truth as I knew myself, and the leaders of the opposition had not taken me into their confidence. It was an ungracious task to inform the high-spirited, uncurbed, and wilful young gentleman that his fellow-students were dissatisfied with him, and that an attempt to run him out of his office was to be made. But Tommy put the question squarely to me, and I could not well avoid the issue. He evidently regarded me as a dependent of the house of Toppleton, whose will could only be the reflection of that of his employers.

"What does it mean? That's what I want to

know," added Tommy, his face lighted up with an excitement which threatened a storm.

"The fellows seem to be disposed to do things as other corporations do," I replied, cautiously, for I did not wish to rouse the sleeping lion in the little lord.

"Wasn't I fair and impartial?" demanded he.

"I think you were," I replied; and I did not lose sight of the fact that he had decided against Barnscott, whose motion he favored, when he gave the floor to Wetherstane.

"The stockholders voted me down just as though they meant to insult me," continued Tommy, smartly. "Do you know why they want to go to Grass Springs to elect officers?"

"For the sake of the dinner, I suppose," I answered. "But, Tommy, there is going to be an opposition to you, at this election."

"An opposition to me!" exclaimed the president, amazed at the intelligence.

"I have only heard it whispered among the fellows."

"What have I done that the fellows should be down upon me?"

"I don't know that I ought to say anything about it, Tommy. It is really none of my business. I shall vote for you."

"If you know anything about it, tell me," continued Tommy, rather imperiously.

"I only know that there is another ticket for directors in the field."

"And my name is not upon it?"

"No, it is not."

Tommy stamped his foot upon the floor, and looked decidedly ugly. I was rather sorry that I had said anything, though it was better for him to be prepared for the result before it was announced.

"Wolf, I don't blame you for this; but I want you to tell me all about it," said he, after he had partially choked down his wrath. "What have I done to set the fellows against me? What do they say about it?"

"They say you put on airs — that you order them around as though you were their master."

"Well, I am president of the road," said he, as if this were a sufficient explanation; and I think he really considered it very unreasonable in the students to object to his conduct.

"I only tell you what the fellows say."

"Wolf, do *you* think I have put on airs?" demanded he.

"So far as I am concerned myself, I haven't a word of fault to find," I replied, evasively.

"You! Well, you are only a hired hand," added he, with refreshing candor. "Do you think I have treated the fellows badly?"

"Not badly; but you know they are rich men's sons, and consider themselves as good as you are."

"But my father built this road, and pays for everything. Not a single one of these fellows ever gave a cent for anything."

"I don't believe the money makes any difference."

"Why don't you say I'm to blame, if you think so?" snapped he, impatiently.

"I believe if you had not been quite so sharp with the fellows they would have liked you better," I answered, desperately. "You tell them to do this and that, and order them just as though they were servants in your father's house. They won't stand it. They are not paid for their work, as I am."

"Thank you; you are very complimentary. I suppose you will call me a tyrant next," sneered he.

"I am only telling you what I have heard the fellows say," I meekly responded.

"Why didn't you tell me this before?" snarled he; and I was fully convinced then, if I had not been before, that honest counsel to such a person is a thankless task.

Tommy walked up and down the hall precisely as his magnificent father would have done, if he had been vexed and disconcerted. I had told him wholesome truth, for which he was not grateful to me.

"Come with me, Wolf," said he, imperiously, after he had considered the matter a while.

The rest of the students were scattered about the building and play-ground of the institute, talking over the meeting, or electioneering for the great occasion, in the afternoon, if Major Toppleton did not veto the proceedings. I followed Tommy over the lawn, where many of the students were assembled in groups. He took no notice of them, unless it was to cast angry and scornful glances at them. He led the way to his father's house, where we found the major in his library.

"Father, we may as well burst up the Lake Shore

Railroad, so far as the students are concerned," said the irate and disgusted president of the company.

"What's the matter now, Tommy?" asked the major, looking up from the newspaper he was reading.

"They are going to run me off the ticket for directors," growled Tommy, dropping heavily into an arm-chair, as though the end of the world had come, and there was nothing more to live for. "They say I have been putting on airs."

"Perhaps you have, Tommy!" suggested the major, who, for some reason or other, was disposed to receive the intelligence very good-naturedly.

"I am the president of the road, and have only done my duty. I'm not going down on my knees to those who are under me."

"But a certain degree of gentlemanly forbearance and consideration is prudent in business relations," added the major. "Now let me hear what the matter is, and we will see what can be done."

Between Tommy and myself we told the great man what had transpired at the hall, and announced the vote of the stockholders, relating to the adjourned meeting and the dinner. The major actually laughed at the impudence of the boys. He was a politic man when policy paid better than violence. There was certainly a breeze among the stockholders of the Lake Shore Railroad. Tommy was in peril of losing his office, which would leave the owner of the road without a suitable representative in the board of directors. The movement must be checked, or the connection of the Institute with the road must be dissolved.

The major was ready to act. The vote of the stockholders was to be carried out in substance. A free train to Grass Spring was to be run at one o'clock; and, at the invitation of the president, a supper was to be served at the hotel after the meeting. This course would conciliate the refractory stockholders, and save the present directors from the accident of being turned out of office. Tommy seemed to be of the opinion that the stockholders ought to be compelled to vote for him, rather than coaxed into it; but he yielded to the superior experience of his father, and consented to feast the electors. He was instructed to invite all the students to the supper, and to have it specially understood that it was his entertainment, not the company's.

There was yet another question to be settled by the students, but not in their capacity as stockholders. The military department of the Institute was still maintained, in spite of the novelty of the rail-road. The boys were organized as a battalion of two companies, and it is hardly necessary to say that Tommy was the major. It was the custom of the Institute to camp out for a week during what was called the home vacation, because the students did *not* generally go home during this period. The stockholders' meeting was held on the Saturday preceding this vacation, and it was necessary to determine where and when the camp should be formed, for this question was left to the students. It was proposed to hold the meeting after the stockholders adjourned, when the major would call the battalion to order.

It was possible, if not probable, that the camping out would be dispensed with the present year, for the new locomotive and cars had just arrived, and were lodged in the houses erected for them. The major had instructed me — or rather the board of directors had done so — to run the new engine on Monday.

It was thought that the students would not be inclined to camp out with this new excitement in store for them.

The road was in order as far as Grass Springs, and in a few weeks it would be completed to Ucayga. I ran regular trips to the former place, every two hours, on the dummy, which was now so degraded by contrast with the locomotive, that it was of small account. But the students did not seem to feel that degree of interest in the new order of things which had been expected. They were excited when the locomotive and cars arrived; shouted, yelled, and screamed till they were hoarse; but the fact that the engine was not to be used as a plaything by any one who desired to do so, operated as a damper upon the boys. Perhaps Tommy, more than any one else, was responsible for this state of things; for his domineering spirit had disgusted his fellow-students.

In my next trip on the dummy Major Toppleton went to Grass Springs, and ordered the supper for the stockholders. At one o'clock I was in the cab of the new locomotive, which, in compliment to the occasion, was to make its first trip to the Springs. It was a beautiful machine, of about two thirds of the ordinary size. The cars were of a corresponding size. Never was an engineer prouder and happier than I was when I ran the engine out of the house. I had borrowed some flags and decorated it for the great occasion. Faxon was with me in the cab, though Lewis Holgate, the son of Christy, who had robbed my father, was employed as fireman.

At the appointed time the students appeared, and, after giving sundry cheers for the train, took their seats, and I started the locomotive. I felt like a real engineer then. The boys screamed as the train moved off, and in half an hour we put on the brakes at Grass Springs. The students hastened to the hotel where the meeting and the supper were to take place. Leaving the engine in charge of Lewis, I hastened to the meeting, where I intended to electioneer for Tommy Toppleton.

CHAPTER IV.

OFF FOR THE CAMP.

"THE time to which this meeting was adjourned has arrived, gentlemen, and you are requested to come to order," said Tommy Toppleton, rapping on the table with the gavel, which he had been careful to bring with him.

"Mr. President," said Barnscott, springing to his feet, with half a dozen others, all anxious to make the first motion.

"Barnscott," replied Tommy, giving him the floor.

"I move you we proceed to the choice of officers."

"Second the motion," added Putnam.

"It is moved and seconded that we proceed to the election of officers," repeated the president.

"Question! Question!" shouted the stockholders; for there was now no difference of opinion on this point.

The motion was carried without opposition. I had intended to make a little speech myself before any business was done. Indeed, it had been arranged by Tommy and his father that I should do so; but Barnscott was too quick for me.

"Mr. President," I shouted, as soon as the vote was declared, "I have a word to say to the stockholders, if you will allow me to speak directly to them."

"Go on! Go on!" yelled the students.

"Gentlemen, though what I have to say does not exactly belong to the business on hand, I hope it won't be taken amiss," I began. "By the vote of the stockholders this morning, the expenses of the supper to be provided for the company at this hotel were to be paid for out of the treasury of the corporation. It is well known that the company is in debt, that the interest on its bonds has not been paid. The president, therefore, in consultation with the munificent patron of the road, did not think it right to use the funds of the company in paying for a supper."

"Are we to have no supper?" demanded Wetherstane.

"We are," I replied, earnestly. "The liberality of the president of the road is well known to all of you, and I have the pleasure of informing you that he has decided to provide the supper at his own expense. It is my pleasant privilege, therefore, to invite you, in behalf of President Toppleton, to a supper at this hotel, after the adjournment. I wish the stockholders especially to understand that this invitation is extended by the president in his private capacity."

Some applause followed my speech; but it was by no means as general and hearty as I desired. It was an electioneering movement, and with this invitation before them, I did not see how the stockholders could well avoid reëlecting Tommy. I saw the leaders of the opposition looking significantly at each other, as though they regarded my movement as a diversion against their scheme. A committee to collect, count, and declare the vote was appointed by the chair, and indorsed by the meeting; and I had the honor to be one of the three..

During the voting, intense excitement prevailed in the hall. It was a general jabber. As far as

my duties would permit, I had been at work for
Tommy. I had used all my powers of persuasion
to induce certain large stockholders to vote for him;
but, as fast as I made an impression, it seemed to
be removed by the opposition, and when the meeting assembled I was not sure that I had converted
a single share, for each of which a vote was given.
But Tommy was reasonably confident of an election.
He threw five hundred votes for himself to begin
with, as the representative of so many shares; and
one more than the same number, in addition, would
elect him. If he could not get so many votes, he
was more unpopular than any of his friends suspected.

"Have all the stockholders voted?" shouted Tommy. "If so, I declare the poll closed!"

The committee retired to sort and count the bal-
lots, taking with us the stock book, in order to
detect any illegal voting. I do not think any
similar occasion among full-grown men excited more
interest and anxiety than this election. Tommy
Toppleton was really on trial for insolence and
tyranny, and the result was to be his acquittal or

conviction. We counted the votes; and Faxon, who was the chairman, and a friend of the president, led the way to the hall, with the result written on a piece of paper in his hand.

"Order, gentlemen!" called Tommy; and his unsteady voice indicated the anxiety with which he waited the issue. "You will listen to the report of the committee."

"Whole number of votes, two thousand," read Faxon, while breathless silence pervaded the hall. "Necessary to a choice, one thousand and one. Thomas Toppleton has eight hundred and eighty-two;" and the chairman read the rest of the names on the same ticket, who had nearly all the vote. "Edward Skotchley has twelve hundred and eighteen."

The chairman then declared that Edward Skotchley, and the others on both tickets, except Tommy, were elected. Some faint applause followed the announcement; but most of the students appeared to be appalled at what they had done. The president's face was as red as a blood beet, and I expected his wrath would boil over. Even the supper

4

had not saved him, and certainly it was a hard case.
I was sorry for him, while I could not approve of
his haughty and overbearing manner. I went up
to the desk with the intention of giving him what
I considered good advice.

"Don't get mad, Tommy," said I, in a low voice,
but so that he could hear me.

"It's an insult," added he, between his closed
teeth.

"Never mind if it is. Don't let them see that
they are punishing you," I added.

This last remark of mine had the desired effect;
and, to my astonishment, he smiled as blandly as
though nothing had happened. He did not relish
the idea of letting his enemies triumph over him,
and though he now looked like peace itself, I was
satisfied that the punishment of the rebels was reserved for another occasion.

"Mr. President!"

Both Tommy and myself looked to see who had
the audacity to break the impressive silence that
still reigned in the hall. It was Skotchley — Edward the Silent, as he was often called, on account
of his quiet way.

" Skotchley," said Tommy, who, though he did not regard his successful rival very favorably, was hypocrite enough to smile sweetly upon him.

" Mr. President, I wish to say that my name was used without my knowledge or consent. I voted for the old board myself, and am so well satisfied with the president, that, even if I considered myself qualified for the position, — which I do not, — I could not accept it."

" Toady!" snuffed some of the students.

Skotchley glanced at the knot of stockholders from whom the offensive word had come. The quiet dignity of his manner silenced them.

" Under no circumstances could I, or would I, accept this office," added Skotchley, as he seated himself, amid the applause of Tommy's friends.

The speaker was not excused; but he adhered to his purpose, and the students were obliged to ballot again. Tommy's singular conduct in not getting mad made a sensation. The students could not comprehend it. While the second ballot was in progress, he sat at the table, cool and smiling. I am satisfied it was this conduct alone which created a reaction in his favor; for on the second ballot he was elected by a majority of one hundred and eleven. He accepted the position, and thanked the stockholders for their continued favor, as coolly as though nothing had occurred to disturb the current of his thoughts.

The present incumbents of the other elective offices were chosen without opposition, and the flurry was over; but it was clear enough, if Tommy did not mend his ways, he would never be elected again. The affairs of the railroad were finished, and those of the battalion were taken up. Tommy was chosen major by a small majority, and the other officers were elected. The location of the encampment caused considerable discussion. Those who had been the leaders of the opposition in the railroad company were in favor of pitching the tents on the Horse Shoe, an island on the lake, opposite Grass Springs, and two miles from the west shore.

Tommy's party advocated the Sandy Bay Grove, because the railroad passed near it. They urged that the Wimpletonians usually encamped on the

Horse Shoe. One of the other side was bold enough to say that was the reason why he wished to go there. I do not know how long the discussion would have lasted if the landlord of the hotel had not given the president a broad hint that the supper was ready. This brought the matter to a crisis, and when the vote was taken, there was a large majority in favor of the Horse Shoe. A committee was appointed to wait upon the owner of the island, who was a resident of Grass Springs.

The landlord of the hotel did justice to himself, and to the great occasion with which his house had been honored. Tommy sat at the head of the middle table, and presided with dignity and discretion. Some very good speeches were made, for boys, and the festival was a decided success. I left the table before the party broke up, in order to have the locomotive ready for the return. At six o'clock we started. Faxon informed me that the Horse Shoe had been engaged for the encampment, and that the sum of ten dollars was to be paid for the use of the island.

"But I can tell you one thing, Wolf. There will be one of the jolliest rows over there that you ever heard of," added Faxon.

"I hope not."

"The Wimpleton fellows were going there; and if there isn't a fight before the week is out, I never will guess again."

"Well, do our fellows know it?" I asked.

"Know it!" exclaimed Faxon. "Of course they do, and that is the particular reason why they want to go there."

"Have the Wimps engaged the island?"

"No; there is where we have the start of them. They have always used it without leave or license."

It did look like an exciting time for the next week. As soon as Tommy Toppleton understood the reason why his battalion had selected the Horse Shoe, he joined heartily with them; for no one hated the Wimpletonians more thoroughly than he did. He entered heart and soul into the project, and issued his order for the march at seven o'clock on Monday morning, so as to reach the island before the enemy could take posses-

THE TOPPLETON BATTALION. — Page 55.

sion of it. I was directed to have the train ready at that hour.

Though it was rather late when we arrived, the boys went to work in making the preparations for the camp, and before they retired, the tents, baggage, and cooking utensils were loaded upon one of the platform cars. Neither the major nor the principal opposed the plan, and at the appointed time on Monday morning, I had the train drawn up on the road at a convenient point near the Institute, ready to furnish the "transportation" for the battalion.

Major Tommy, intent upon being ahead of the enemy on the other side of the lake, was on time with his force. The battalion was to be reviewed by the principal of the Institute before its departure, and the two companies marched by the train, on their way to the green where the ceremony was to take place. As they passed me, I saluted them with the steam whistle, and in return the warlike heroes cheered the train. I witnessed the impressive formalities of the review, and having moved the cars forward, I heard the speech of the principal at the close of the performance.

The students then entered the cars. I gave a tremendous whistle, and off we went, the students, true to their noisy natures, yelling like madmen. As we moved on, we discovered a fleet of boats, loaded with Wimpletonians, sailing down the lake.

CHAPTER V.

BREEZY PROSPECT AHEAD.

I AM not quite sure that Major Toppleton did not know the Wimpletonians had selected the Horse Shoe for their camp ground, and that a collision was likely to occur between the students of the rival academies. If he did know it, he was certainly to blame, even though the Toppletonians had legal possession of the land; for a man is morally responsible far beyond the letter of the law. It was plain enough to me that the wire-pullers on our side had selected the Horse Shoe simply because it was the usual encampment of their rivals.

The Toppletonians were highly excited and intensely belligerent. The jealousy between the two sides of the lake and between the two schools had thoroughly infected them. There were only a few who were not ready to fight for the banner under which they marched. While I confess that I was to some extent a partisan for the Toppletonians, I could not help feeling that there was something undignified and unmanly in this senseless quarrel. I could realize this sentiment, even while I was anxious that the Wimpletonians should not "get ahead" of our side. I was not in love with Colonel Wimpleton and his son, but I should have preferred to treat them with dignified contempt, rather than pick a quarrel with them.

The Wimpletonians had a whole fleet of boats, including the dozen or more that belonged to the Institute, and several bateaux, loaded with tents and baggage. The wind was light early in the day, and as they had to sail a dozen miles before they reached their destination, they were not likely to arrive at the island before us. Major Toppleton had ordered the tug steamer to be at Grass Springs to convey the students to the Horse Shoe, and she had towed a number of boats for the use of the battalion.

"We must hurry up, Wolf," said Faxon, who, as usual, was on the engine with me, after glancing at the aquatic procession on the lake.

"It will take the Wimps three hours to reach the Horse Shoe with this breeze," I replied. "Our party will arrive in an hour."

"There may be some delay at the Springs. We don't know that the steamer will be there when we arrive."

"Didn't Major Toppleton send her to the Springs?" I asked, not being aware that there was any contingency.

"He sent her to Ucayga last night with a freight of flour, and told Captain Underwood to be at Grass Springs at eight o'clock, if possible. She may be late. She did not leave Middleport till dark, and of course she must discharge her cargo this morning. If there should be no steamer ready for us, what shall we do?"

"Where are our boats?" I inquired.

"I suppose Captain Underwood left them at the wharf at the Springs, as he passed, or possibly at the Horse Shoe. I only know what Tommy told me, just before we started."

"There is a chance for a slip, after all," I added.

"I think there is a big chance for a slip. If the

Wimps get to the island first, there will be a big fight, for our fellows don't wish for any better fun than driving them off."

"And perhaps the Wimps would like no better fun than that of driving the Tops off."

"Possession is nine points, you know, and the side which gets a footing on the island first has the best chance," replied Faxon, cheerfully; and though he did not bluster so much as some others, I knew that he was "ready to go his length" in opposition to the enemy.

"It looks like a fight, any way you can fix it," I added. "Why couldn't our fellows have chosen some other place to encamp?"

"Because the Horse Shoe suits them best. There is a good wharf at the island, and plenty of dry wood for the fires."

"I don't see the use of quarrelling when there are a hundred other places just as good as that."

"What's the matter, Wolf? Have you no stomach for a fight?" laughed Faxon.

"No; I have not."

"But you are regarded by the fellows as a regular

fighting-cock. Your affairs with Waddie and with —"
Faxon checked himself, as he glanced at Lewis Holgate, the fireman —" you know whom, are the foun-
dation of your popularity with them."

"I am willing to fight in a good cause; but I don't
believe in bringing on a quarrel."

" The Wimps are always picking upon us, and
doing us mischief whenever they can. They have
torn up our track once, and we haven't paid them
off for that."

"You sunk all their boats for that; and I think
you are about even."

"Not quite; but if they will let us alone, we won't
meddle with them. We have hired the Horse Shoe
for the week, and we mean to have it. We have
the legal right to the island, and we are ready to
fight for possession."

"I think it is all nonsense to quarrel for nothing."

"We shall have the fun of licking them."

"Or the fun of being licked," I suggested.

"No danger of that. We have one hundred and
fifteen students now, and I was told that the Wimps
had fallen off to less than a hundred," chuckled
Faxon.

" The tables may be turned by and by, when the colonel's plans are in operation."

" What plans? " asked my companion, anxiously.

" You did not suppose Colonel Wimpleton would permit this railroad scheme to·go on without doing something to offset it — did you? " I replied ; and I had received some positive information from my father, the night before, on this interesting topic.

" What can he do? He can't build a railroad on his side of the lake."

"No; but at this moment Waddie Wimpleton is the president of a corporation."

" What corporation ? "

" A steamboat company."

" Is that so ? "

" My father was over at Centreport yesterday, and found out all about it."

" But what have the Wimps to do with it ? "

" The colonel is building a magnificent little steamer at Hitaca. She is to be very long and narrow, and good for fifteen to eighteen miles an hour. The Institute fellows on the other side are to own and manage her, just as you do the railroad."

"That is news, certainly," said Faxon, musing, and apparently not at all pleased with the plan.

"They say Major Toppleton has bought up the steamers which now run on the lake, and means to take them off between Ucayga and Middleport as soon as the Lake Shore Railroad is completed."

"Of course; what's the use of having the boats after the road is finished? We are to run a LIGHTNING EXPRESS twice a day then, and I think it is very good-natured of the major to buy up the boats, and thus save the owners from loss."

"Perhaps it is; but is it good-natured for him to deprive the Centreporters of the means of getting to Ucayga, as he will when the boats are taken off?"

"They can go by the railroad, the same as others," laughed Faxon.

"They can, but they won't. Do you think Colonel Wimpleton would come over here and ride in these cars? He would hang himself first."

"Then he can hang himself, if he likes. The Middleporters wouldn't cry if he did."

"But he intends neither to hang himself nor to ride on the Lake Shore Railroad. Of course you can't blame him for kicking against the movements of the major."

"See here, Wolf; are you a Wimp or a Top?" demanded Faxon, coloring a little, as we looked into each other's face.

"Why do you ask that question?" I inquired, quietly.

"Just now you seemed to stick up for the Wimpleton side."

"I was only stating the case just as it is. My sympathies are on this side; but I don't blame Colonel Wimpleton for not being willing to have his facilities for going to and from Ucayga cut off."

"You don't blame him!"

"Certainly not."

"I believe you are only half a Top now, Wolf. Just now you were condemning us for standing up for our own rights. Be on one side or the other, old fellow."

"I am willing to fight for the side that gives me bread and butter, as long as it stands by the right."

"I don't like this making reservations. I go the

whole figure. My country, right or wrong — that's what I go for."

"So do I. My country, right or wrong; if wrong, to set her right."

"There you spoil all the poetry of the thing. If you had stopped before you put the last sentence on, it would have been just the thing. I go for Toppleton, right or wrong."

"I don't," I replied, decidedly. "I am for keeping Toppleton right, and then I go for Toppleton."

"What's the use of talking, Wolf! You can't make me believe you are not right on the goose," added Faxon, good-naturedly. "When will that magnificent steamer be launched?"

"I don't know; but father said the hull was nearly completed. I suppose they can't get her ready for service before August or September; perhaps not till next spring."

"And then she is to run in opposition to the Lake Shore Railroad?"

"That's the idea, I believe."

"There will be jolly times then; but she can't do anything against our lightning express."

5

" I'm not so sure of that."

" Come, Wolf! You are a Wimp at heart, after all. The fellows would mob you if they should hear you sticking up for the other side," added Faxon.

" I'm not sticking up for the other side," I replied, smartly, for I did not relish this charge. " I'm only looking the facts fair in the face. The Wimps' steamer will give you a hard run. Look at it for yourself."

" I don't believe the Wimps can get ahead of us, any how — I won't believe it!" persisted Faxon.

" How far is it from Middleport to Ucayga? " I asked.

" Twenty miles, to a rod."

" How long will it take the lightning express to go through ? "

" Half an hour," replied Faxon, sharply.

" Not much ! We should have a smash every day at that rate. The track is not stiff enough to make that time upon. Call it forty minutes; and that is high speed for this light rail."

" Well, forty minutes. You don't mean to say any steamer can make twenty miles in that time ? "

" Hold on a minute ! How wide is the river at Ucayga ? "

" Half a mile."

" Good ; we have to land our passengers on this side of the river. To take the trains east and west, they must cross the river, and do the same when they visit the town. How long will that take in the old sail-boat ferry ? "

" I don't know," replied Faxon, nettled by the force of the argument, which he could not answer.

" Half an hour, at least, on an average. That will make an hour and ten minutes; and the steamer will do it in an hour and a quarter. I think the colonel has a pretty good show," I continued, as the train reached Spangleport, and I blew some desperate whistles to warn idlers about the track.

" You are a Wimp ! "

" No. I'm a Top."

" Don't talk so before the other fellows. If you do they will think you have sold out to the enemy."

" Can't a fellow express an honest opinion ? " I asked, warmly.

" Not when it don't jibe with the public sentiment."

" I don't know about that. I'm not afraid to tell
Major Toppleton what I think."

" Don't you do it."

"If he wants to come out ahead, as of course he
does, it would be better for him to look the facts
and contingencies fairly in the face."

Faxon was thinking of the matter, and by mutual
consent both of us were silent.

CHAPTER VI.

A MISSION OF PEACE.

I COULD not exactly see that I was a traitor to the Toppletonian interest because I believed that a steamer could successfully compete even with a "lightning express." I intended to serve my employers faithfully, and believed that I had done so. Perhaps it was imprudent for me to express an opinion; but I knew that Colonel Wimpleton was a man of energy and determination, and that he would not be content to remain long in the shade.

I observed that Lewis Holgate listened very attentively to all that was said, though he made no remarks. Since his father had run away with the money he had stolen, the family were hard pressed to get a living. Lewis was about my own age, and was regarded as a smart fellow. The intimacy between our families had brought us together some-

what, and I knew that he aspired to be a "young
engineer." He had worked with his father a great
deal, and knew an engine very well. It was necessary for him to go to work, to assist in supporting
his mother and his brothers and sisters. He had
told me how sorry he was for what his father had
done, and I pitied him. Through my influence he
had obtained the place to "fire" on the new locomotive, and now received a salary of three dollars
a week.

Lewis worked with me a while on the dummy, and
was competent to run it. The crime of his father
had to some extent broken his spirit, and thus far
he had behaved very well, better than his antece-
dents led me to expect — for he had been rather
noted in Ucayga as a bad boy. My mother com-
mended me warmly for what I had done to help
him, and declared she was very glad to see me
manifest a Christian spirit towards him. My father
said I was foolish to try to serve such a fellow;
but I was best satisfied with the judgment of my
mother.

Something had already been said about another

locomotive, and an additional number of freight and passenger cars, which the business of the road would eventually demand. Lewis Holgate gave me to understand that the height of his ambition was to be the engineer of the new locomotive when it came. I assured him that if he did his duty faithfully, I would do all I could to further his purpose. We were, therefore, good friends, and I gave him every facility for learning the business. If I had had any doubts about the propriety of what I had said to Faxon, for which he had accused me of being a Wimp, I should not have restrained my speech on account of the presence of Lewis; for, after all I had done for him, I did not think him capable of injuring me.

"The tug steamer is not here," said Faxon, as I shut off the steam when the train approached Grass Springs.

"It isn't eight o'clock yet. We have been only half an hour on the road," I replied.

"I don't believe it will be here," added Faxon, anxiously, as he looked out upon the waters of the lake. "There is a stiff breeze now, and the Wimps will be here by nine o'clock."

I could not see why my partisan friend should manifest any anxiety, since he and the rest of the Toppletonians, with a few exceptions, were absolutely spoiling for a fight with their rivals on the other side of the lake. The train approached the Grass Springs station, and I whistled to put on the brakes. As soon as we stopped, Faxon left the engine, and the battalion came out of the cars. The two companies formed on the wharf, and I heard sharp and imperative orders of Major Tommy, which led me to conclude that his experience in the stockholders' meeting had not been very profitable to him, though some of the harshness of his tones was doubtless attributable to his military enthusiasm.

From my place in the cab I could see the end of the lake, with the steeples of Ucayga in the distance; but the steamer was not on the way; she had not even started for the Springs. The Horse Shoe was two miles from the shore. The wind had freshened a little, and was fair for boats coming down the lake. The battalion from Centreport must arrive in an hour, or an hour and a half at the farthest, for the boats had had only ten miles to make half an hour before. Major Tommy had formed his lines; the quartermaster had placed all the baggage and stores on the wharf, and everything was in readiness to embark. It was eight o'clock by this time, and the steamer had not yet appeared. The Toppleton boats had probably been left at the island, for they were not to be found at the main shore, and the steamer could have left them with less delay than at the Grass Springs Wharf.

" What's to be done?" asked Major Tommy, impatiently, after he had surveyed the ground over and over again.

" We must get to the island some how or other," replied Faxon.

" That steamer won't be here for an hour," growled the commander of the battalion. " Father said it might be late ; but he didn't understand exactly what was up."

" The Wimps are coming," shouted an officer in the line.

" They are five miles off," replied Faxon, as he looked up the lake. " I want to be on the island when they come."

"So do I," replied Tommy, casting an anxious glance at the approaching enemy.

"Can't you help us out, Wolf?" asked the major, jumping on the foot-board of the engine.

Of course I was well pleased to be called upon in the emergency, for it was manifesting a great deal of confidence to ask advice of a boy who was not a member of the battalion. The Toppletonians had the legal right to use the Horse Shoe; and it seemed to me that, if they had possession of the island when the Wimpletonians arrived, the anticipated fight, at least as a brutal struggle, might be averted. Both bodies were armed with small muskets, having bayonets upon them; and though they were not allowed any amunition, they might make the combat more dangerous than they intended. The interests of peace, therefore, appeared to require that our battalion should be transported to the island without delay.

"I hope you are not going to get up a fight over there," I ventured to say.

"Of course we are not, if the Wimps let us alone," replied Tommy. "If they don't let us alone, it will be the worse for them. I want to get over there before they do, and that steamer, confound it, won't be here this hour."

"If I were you, Tommy, I would send one company over to the island, and take possession of it, leaving the baggage and tents to be carried over when the steamer comes."

"How can I send one company over?" snapped Tommy. "We haven't a boat, or even a mud-scow."

"There comes the ferry-boat," I replied, pointing to a sloop-rigged craft which was now approaching the shore from Ruoara, on the other side and above the island.

"That's the idea!" exclaimed Tommy, as he leaped down from the cab, and ran with a speed entirely beneath the dignity of the major of a battalion to the ferry pier.

In three minutes more he had made a trade with the ferryman to land as many of the force as his boat would accommodate on the Horse Shoe. The craft was one peculiar to the lakes in that region. It was an ordinary sloop, though rather longer than

similar vessels are built; but the stern was open just
above the water-line, so that teams could be driven
on board. It depended upon the wind as its pro-
pelling agent, though it was provided with a pair
of steamboat wheels, with a horse-power machine to
turn them, which could be used when the wind was
not available.

Major Tommy ordered Captain Briscoe, with Company A, to embark in this ferry-boat, and to hold
the Horse Shoe, at any peril, until the other company could be sent over. I was sorry to leave the
exciting scene; but I had to run the trip from
Middleport at nine o'clock. Satisfied that the Toppletonians would secure possession of the island
before the arrival of the enemy, I turned the locomotive, and ran back to the other terminus. The
fleet of boats was off the South Shoe, not more than
a mile from the Horse Shoe, when the train went
through Spangleport; but the ferry-boat was within
half that distance of its destination.

We did not yet run the new locomotive and cars
on the regular trips, because the travel was light,
and the dummy could be used at half the expense.

We housed the engine and cars, and, firing up the dummy, we had steam enough to start her at the appointed hour. Just before we left, Major Toppleton came into the station, and asked me what had become of the students. I told him I had conveyed them to Grass Springs.

"I did not know they were going so early," added he.

"They were in a hurry," I replied, with a smile, when I saw that the great man did not comprehend the strategy of the battalion. "My orders from Major Tommy were to start at seven o'clock; and I set them down on the wharf at the Springs at half past seven."

"You look wiser than you speak, Wolf," said the major, gazing earnestly into my face. "Is there any mischief brewing?"

"I think there is," I replied, candidly, though I could not help smiling at the puzzled look of the magnate of Middleport.

"What is it? Why didn't you tell me about it? They say the students of the Wimpleton Institute went down the lake this morning."

"Yes, sir; we passed them on the way, and the students of both Institutes are bound to the same place."

"Then there will be a quarrel!" exclaimed the major; but I think he would not have cared if he had been sure that his side of the lake would be victorious.

"I am afraid there will; but the Toppletonians have the weather-gage, both on the rights of the case and in the situation."

I explained fully what had transpired at the meeting of the battalion on Saturday, and the state of the affair when I left Grass Springs, an hour before.

"Why didn't they tell me what they were doing?" demanded the major. "I did not know they were in a hurry; if I had, the steamer should have been at Grass Springs without fail. If our boys have hired the Horse Shoe, and pay for it, they have a right to use it."

The great man was unequivocally on the side of the boys, and they might just as well have taken him into their confidence. I was sorry to see him so willing to permit a collision, even while our students had the letter of the law in their favor.

"Wolf, don't you want a vacation?" said the major, suddenly turning to me, after musing on the facts I had given him.

"No, sir; I don't care about any," I replied.

"But I prefer that you should take one. Your pay shall go on as usual," he continued; and of course it was of no use for me to protest. "Can Lewis run the dummy?"

"Yes, sir; he understands it very well."

"All right, Wolf; I want you to be with those boys. You have an influence with them, and they want some help such as you can give them."

"Am I to fight with them, sir?" I asked, laughing; for I did not exactly relish the kind of vacation he intended to give me.

"Certainly I don't want any fighting if it can be avoided. I want you to help keep the peace. If things don't work well, or any help is needed, come to me at once."

I started the dummy, and then gave it up to

Lewis. I did not exactly like my mission; for, though I was sent to keep the peace, I knew that the major simply expected me to see that the Toppletonians were not whipped in the expected encounter.

CHAPTER VII.

MAJOR TOMMY GETS MAD.   •

THOUGH I was nominally sent to the Horse Shoe as an ambassador of peace, I fully understood the real object of the magnate in giving me a vacation. The mission was certainly complimentary to me, for I was really expected to do the "engineering" for the Toppletonians. I was not to permit them to be whipped by their great enemy: if I could not prevent it myself, I was to call in the assistance of Major Toppleton. Whatever instructions he may have given me, this was precisely what he meant. I was, in some sense, to be his representative.

I desired to keep the peace, and I hoped to have influence enough to accomplish something in this direction; but it would not be an easy matter to do this, and at the same time escape the wrath

6

of the belligerent Toppletonians. The Wimpleton battalion, under command of Major Waddie, would be ten times as reckless as the Toppletonians under Major Tommy. My late enemy on the other side was not restrained either by fear or by principle. No violence or destruction appalled him. His father had so often paid for damage done by him, that he never hesitated to gratify his malice and revenge by smashing a boat, firing a building, or even discharging his pistol at any one who thwarted him. He was a dangerous enemy. But Waddie was reckless only when he was personally in a safe position. He was prudent enough to keep his own body out of the way of harm, except when his wrath completely mastered him.

Lewis Holgate was glad enough of an opportunity to run the dummy alone, for it would enable him to prove his fitness for the position to which he aspired. I cautioned him carefully in regard to keeping up the water in the boiler, and the pressure of steam he might carry. He was very passive and tractable, and, for the sake of his own reputation, I had no doubt he would be faithful and careful in the discharge of his duty.

When I arrived at Grass Springs in the dummy, the steamer was just approaching the wharf. The company sent over to the island under Captain Briscoe had landed, and thus far had held peaceful possession. The Horse Shoe was the most western of four islands, just below Ruoara. The two largest of them lay east and west of each other, while the one to the north of them was called the North Shoe, and the one to the south the South Shoe. They bore some resemblance to shoes; and the western island having a bay which made into its southern side, gave it the shape of a horse shoe. The eastern island, and the nearest to the shore, looked more like a pistol than either of the others did like the articles for which they were named. But the person who had christened the group, having probably named the others first, calling each a shoe, designated the fourth the "Shooter," instead of the Pistol, which would have been more appropriate. "Shoe" and "Shooter" seemed to jingle well with him, and, as he was satisfied, I shall not complain.

The squadron of boats from Centreport lay be-

tween the Horse Shoe and the South Shoe when
I came upon the ground. So far as I could judge
by seeing them at the distance of two miles, the
Wimpletonians were consulting upon their next
movement. If they intended to take possession
of the island, they had permitted the favorable
opportunity to pass. Doubtless they were also
waiting for the arrival of the bateaux, on which
their baggage was transported.

"Has anything happened?" I asked of Faxon,
as I joined the students on the wharf.

"Not a thing!" exclaimed he. "The Wimps
smell a mice, and don't seem to be inclined to
pitch in. If I had been Waddie Wimpleton, I
would have landed on that island before this time."

Faxon appeared to be disappointed because the
row had not come off, and more, perhaps, because
the Wimpletonians did not display a belligerent spirit.
The steamer came up to the wharf, and the students embarked. Major Tommy stormed at Captain Underwood for his delay, and the poor captain
defended himself very modestly and gently. He
had discharged his cargo as speedily as possible,

and he had not been told to be at the Springs at eight, but as soon as he could. His bread and butter depended upon keeping the right side of the magnate, and to prejudice the son was to influence the father.

"What are you doing here, Wolf?" asked Tommy, as he saw me standing on the forward deck, after the steamer started.

"Your father has just given me a vacation," I replied, very quietly; for I did not deem it prudent to put on any airs about my mission. "I thought I would come over and see how this thing was coming out."

"It's coming out all right, Wolf. What did my father say?" asked the little major, with some show of anxiety. "Was he mad because we came away so early?"

"O, no! I told him where you were going, and that the Wimps were bound to the same place. He was very glad you had obtained permission of the owner to use the island."

"Then it is all right — is it, Wolf?" added Tommy, with an apparent feeling of relief. "I didn't know but my governor sent you here as a spy. If he did, you can return as fast as you came."

Perhaps, according to Tommy's interpretation of my mission, I might be a spy. I had really been sent to act as a check upon the students, who were very jealous of any interference when they were on camp duty, or any other military service. The steamer sped on its way, and as the deep water was between the Horse Shoe and the Shooter, we had to round the southern point of the former in order to reach the landing-place. The Wimpleton boats still lay off the South Shoe, and Captain Underwood said they were in the channel through which he must pass.

"Can't you get to the landing without going near them?" I asked privately of the captain, though I knew the navigation of the lake as well as he did.

"I can go to the north of the Horse Shoe, and come down the channel in that way," he replied.

"These fellows are spoiling for a fight, and I am afraid there will be some broken heads before the day is finished. If you can prevent a row, it will be better to do it."

"Very well," said he, ringing the bell to stop her, just as he was entering the channel between the Horse Shoe and the South Shoe.

"What's that for?" demanded Major Tommy from the forward deck.

"Don't you think we had better go in at the northward of the island?" inquired Captain Underwood, with the utmost deference.

"No, sir! I don't think so!" replied Tommy, warmly. "Are you going the other way because those boats are here? Go ahead, sir! Run them down, if they don't get out of the way!"

Captain Underwood felt obliged to obey this imperative order. If he had refused to do so, it is quite likely he would have been compelled to return to the skippership of a canal boat, from which he had been promoted to his present more dignified and lucrative position.

"Don't run them down, captain," I ventured to say, in a low tone, as the master rang the bell to go ahead again.

"It is hard work to please that boy without getting into trouble," added the captain. "The good book says no man can serve two masters, but I have to serve two."

"Blow the whistle, captain!" I suggested.

He blew the whistle till the shores resounded with the echoing screeches; but the Wimpletonians evidently believed the steamer had come this way on purpose to annoy them, and they stood upon their dignity. Not a boat moved, and the students in them looked as resolute as though they meant to be smashed rather than change their position. We were almost upon them, and I was afraid the captain intended to execute the barbarous threat of Major Tommy. I begged him again not to run into the boats; and seeing the enemy did not mean to move, he stopped and backed in season to avoid a calamity.

"What did you stop for, captain?" shouted Tommy; but I was charitable enough to believe that the words were intended for the benefit of the Wimpletonians, rather than the person to whom they were addressed.

Captain Underwood made no reply, but rang to go ahead again, though he permitted but two or three turns of the wheels.

"I can shove the boats out of the way without hurting any one, I think," said he, as the steamer moved slowly forward.

"Look out, or you will run into us!" shouted my old enemy, Ben Pinkerton, who was in the nearest boat.

"Out of the way, then!" replied Captain Underwood.

"Go ahead, full steam, captain!" called Tommy; but again I wished to believe that his order was a threat to the enemy rather than an indication of a wicked purpose.

Instead of obeying this rash command, the captain rang the bell to back her, fearful that some of the boats might be smashed.

I saw Tommy rush aft, and I supposed he intended to come upon the hurricane deck, where he could bully Captain Underwood more effectually. I left the wheel-house, where I had been during the conversation with the captain, that he might

not implicate me in the disobedience. But Tommy
did not appear, and it was plain that he had adopted some other tactics.

"Wolf Penniman!" shouted some one at the
gangway. "You are wanted below!"

"What is wanted?" I asked of the messenger,
who could hardly speak, he was so excited.

"Major Toppleton wants you."

I went below, and found Major Tommy standing
at the door of the engine-room, foaming with wrath;
indeed, he had steam enough on to carry a forty-
horse engine.

"Will you do as I tell you, or not?" stormed
Tommy, addressing his energetic words to the engineer.

"You must excuse me, Mr. Tommy; but I must
mind the bells. It won't do for me to disobey the
captain's orders," protested the engineer, gently and
respectfully.

"Here, Wolf!" shouted Tommy. "Come here!"

I presented myself to the little magnate, and I
was conscious that I was already in a bad scrape.

"Go in there, and start up that engine! Go ahead,
full steam!" continued he.

I looked at him, but I did not move to obey. I smiled, and looked as good-natured as possible, for I did not wish him to think that I was ugly about it.

"Don't you hear me, Wolf? I tell you to start up that engine!" repeated Major Tommy.

"It won't do for me to step in between the man and his engine," I remonstrated, mildly.

"Yes, it will! I tell you to do it; and if you don't do it, you shall suffer for it."

"Let us argue the point a little, major," I replied.

"Will you do what I tell you, or not?" roared he, swelling up as big as a major general.

"You must excuse me, major, but I can't take the engine out of the engineer's hands, without the captain's orders."

"I will let you know that this boat is my father's, and I can do with it as I please. If you won't start it, I will do so myself!" said the juvenile magnate, desperately, as he rushed into the engine-room, and seized hold of the working-bar.

"You musn't touch the engine," said the man in charge, as he took hold of Tommy's arm, and, with as little force as was necessary, thrust him out of the room.

Tommy was the maddest major I ever saw.

CHAPTER VIII.

CHARGE BAYONETS !

MAJOR TOMMY, in my judgment, was more inclined to have his own way than he was to annihilate the Wimpletonians by crushing them under the wheels of the steamer. He had been irritated because the captain did not obey his order; but, I think, if the boat had gone ahead at his imperial command, he would have been the first to stop her. I could not believe that he was so diabolically wicked as to run over the boats, and sacrifice the lives of a dozen or more even of his enemies. If it had been Waddie, the matter would have been different, and I should have been more credulous.

When the captain opposed him, he flew to the engineer; but I am confident that, if the man had given the wheel a single turn, Tommy would have ordered him to stop her. Neither the captain nor the engineer knew that he did not intend to do all he threatened; and I am afraid, if the wheels had been started, the mischief would have been done, whatever the little magnate meant, or did not mean. I was very sorry to be dragged into the difficulty, for Tommy and I had thus far been very good friends. However, I had no doubts in regard to the correctness of my position.

Forbush, the engineer, had gently, very gently, thrust Tommy out of the engine-room. By this time, all of Company B had gathered around the little major, intent upon beholding the row. The juvenile magnate was boiling over with rage, and threatened Captain Underwood, the engineer, and myself with total annihilation. Every one of us should lose his situation, and be forever deprived of the power to obtain further employment.

"Come, Tommy, keep cool," said Faxon, trying to smooth down the wrinkled fur on the badger's back.

"I won't keep cool! I have been insulted, and I will teach the fellows who and what I am. If I tell the captain of this boat to run over the island, he shall do it," stormed Tommy, so angry that he could hardly keep from crying.

"Be reasonable, Tommy," added Skotchley, with his usual quiet dignity. "We don't want to kill anybody."

"Yes, we do! We want to kill the Wimps if they don't get out of the way."

It was useless to say anything to the irate major while he was so inflamed with wrath, and by general consent the students kept still; but they were disgusted with the commander of the battalion, and doubtless most of them were sorry that they had not tipped him out of both of his offices. While Tommy was still raving like an insane person, the bell rang again to go ahead, and the engineer promptly started the wheels; but only a few turns were made before the signal came to stop her. Finding I was not needed on the main deck, and that the wrathful major would cool off sooner if left to himself, I went up to the wheel-house. All on board, except the captain and one man at the wheel, had been attracted to the vicinity of the engine-room by the exciting scene. There was no one on the forward deck, for even the two men employed there were listening to the howls of Tommy.

Captain Underwood had started the boat ahead again, and when I reached the wheel-house, she was gently crowding her way through the fleet of boats, a dozen in number, containing the whole force of the Wimpletonians, over ninety of them. She struck the boats as gingerly as though they had been eggs. She did them no harm, beyond scraping the fresh paint upon them, as she slowly forced her way through them. I watched the movement with interest, for I was curious to know what the Wimpletonians intended to do.

The fleet lay in the deep water, so that there was no room on either side for the steamer to pass to her destination without getting aground. Captain Underwood was a prudent man, and worked his craft very carefully. He had given her headway enough to carry her through the squadron of boats; but, as they swarmed along her bow, and under her guards, the students in them fastened to her with their boat-hooks, so that they could not be shaken off.

" Back her quick, and you will shake them off

without harming any of them," I suggested to the captain, when I saw that he was nettled by the failure of his plan.

" Out of the way there ! Your boats will be smashed under our wheels ! " shouted he to the enemy.

At that moment half a dozen of the Wimpletonians leaped over the rail of the steamer upon the forward deck, with their muskets in their hands.

" What's that for ? " said the captain, quietly.

" They mean mischief," I replied, as I saw a dozen more follow the six ; and among the latter was Waddie Wimpleton, glittering with gold lace, for he was in the full uniform of a major of infantry.

" Stand by those two doors ! " shouted he, drawing his sword and pointing to the entrances near which the Toppletonians were still listening to the howlings of Major Tommy. " Hurry up, there ! " he added to those in the boats.

The Wimpletonians poured in over the 'rail, until the deck was crowded. Company B had stacked their muskets on this deck, and except the officers, our boys were unarmed, while every Wimpletonian

7

presented a musket with a fixed bayonet upon it.
As the enemy were boarding the steamer, the captain, amazed at the audacity of the young ruffians,
rang the bell to back the boat; but before she had
headway enough to shake off the fleet, which clung
to her like swarming bees, all the Wimpletonians,
except one in each boat, were on our deck.

"Up there, twenty of you!" said Major Waddie,
indicating the hurricane deck with a flourish of his
sword.

"What are the rascals going to do?" added
Captain Underwood, who had not given the enemy
credit for the skill and daring they now displayed.

"Don't let a single Top go on the hurricane
deck!" shouted Waddie; and the twenty students
he had sent up stationed themselves at the head of
the stairs, to prevent any of our party from leaving their prison; for such it had now become to
them.

Captain Underwood began to think the frolic, as
he had at first regarded it, was becoming a serious
affair, and I saw that he looked somewhat anxious.
Our fellows had left their muskets on the forward

CHARGE BAYONETS! — Page 98.

deck, and they were now in possession of the enemy. I am inclined to think it was fortunate they were there, rather than in the hands of their owners, or some of the students on both sides would doubtless have been seriously injured. As the matter now stood, the Wimpletonians had entire possession of the Middleport, for that was the name of the steamer. Twenty of them stood in the act of charging bayonets in the direction of the two doors leading from the forward deck. Our fellows could do nothing; and even the captain, with the wheel in his hand, was as powerless as they were.

Major Waddie, with his chapeau and white plume, looked as though he were the commander-in-chief of a great army, and had just achieved a bloody victory. I must do him the justice to say that he had managed the affair very well, though I saw that his two captains, Dick Bayard and Ben Pinkerton, were always near him with words of counsel. I was at a loss to determine whether the capture of the steamer had been devised on the instant, or whether the boats had taken the position in the channel for that purpose in the beginning. I was inclined to believe that the bold step was first suggested when their leaders saw the muskets of the Toppletonians stacked on the forward deck, and not a single soldier present to guard them. Ben Pinkerton afterwards told me that this view was correct.

While the conquerors were disposing their forces so as to hold the prize they had captured, Major Tommy and the audience who were listening to his angry declamation were completely intrapped. The startling event was calculated to turn the spouter's thoughts into a new channel. It seemed to me that the emergency had arisen which would justify me in calling the attention of Major Toppleton to the affair; but unfortunately I could not leave just then. The steamer had backed half a mile from the island, and had now shaken off all the boats which clung to her.

"I don't know what these ruffians intend to do," said Captain Underwood, as he rang the bell to stop her.

"Waddie Wimpleton is reckless enough to do almost anything," I replied; for I regarded the situation as difficult, if not dangerous.

"I will keep the boat moving towards Middleport, at any rate."

"That's right, captain; if they have us, we have them at the same time, and we can carry them to Middleport as prisoners of war," I added, with a smile which was not wholly natural.

Captain Underwood rang the bell to go ahead, and soon gave her full speed, heading the boat up the lake.

"Hallo, there!" shouted Major Waddie from the forward deck, as he flourished his sword towards the wheel-house. "Stop her!"

The captain paid no attention to this imperious command.

"Do you hear me? I say, stop her!" yelled Waddie.

"Hold your tongue, you little bantam!" replied Captain Underwood, irreverently; for, as he owed no allegiance to the house of Wimpleton, he felt that he could afford to speak without measuring his words.

"Will you obey me, or not?" demanded Waddie, furious because his imperious will was not regarded.

But the two captains, who were really the brains of the battalion, interposed. I do not know what they said, but the major with the chapeau desisted from his attempt to bully the captain. They were more practical in their operations than the commander, and presently I saw them forming their forces before the two doors. Captain Bayard drew up his company before one of them, and Captain Pinkerton before the other.

"Charge bayonets!" said Waddie, fiercely.

The order was repeated by the two captains, who placed their most reliable men in the front.

"Forward!" screamed Major Waddie, making a desperate lunge into the empty air with his flashing sword.

"Forward!" repeated the two captains, as they drove their men through the doors, into the narrow space on each side of the boiler and engine-room.

The Toppletonians were in these spaces, and I saw that the object of the movement was to drive them aft, and get possession of the engine-room, so as to control the machinery, and thus prevent the captain from taking the boat to Middleport.

Our fellows, unarmed, could not stand up against the bayonets of the enemy, and we heard them fall back. I concluded, by this time, that Major Tommy had come to his senses; though, if he was disposed still further to vent his ire, he had an excellent opportunity to do so against the sharp-pointed weapons of his conquerors.

The Toppletonians were not only driven aft, but were forced below the deck into the little cabin, which was hardly large enough to hold them all. A little later, we heard a violent altercation in the engine-room, and then the boat stopped. The Wimpletonians had certainly won a complete victory.

CHAPTER IX.

FEATHERS AND THE ENGINEER.

MAJOR TOMMY TOPPLETON and Company B were prisoners in the little cabin, while Major Waddie Wimpleton and Companies A and B of his battalion were in possession of the steamer. The wheels had stopped, and this was evidence to us in the wheel-house that Forbush, the engineer, had been driven from his post.

"This will never do," said Captain Underwood. "The young rascals will blow us all up. They have stopped the engine, and have not let off steam."

Though it was really becoming quite a serious matter, I saw that the captain could hardly keep from laughing, there was something so absurd in the situation. Major Waddie, in his chapeau and gold lace, strutted before us on the forward deck, and we had regarded the whole affair as a joke; but now we were actually in the toils of the captors. They had not yet disturbed the occupants of the wheel-house; but this step had only been deferred till the other parts of the boat were made secure. The Toppletonians had all been locked up in the cabin, and the engine-room, the citadel of the boat, had yielded.

"It is time something was done," I replied to the captain. "I have been opposed to a fight, but I think one is necessary about this time."

"What shall we do?"

"That's the question. The Wimpletonians are armed with ugly weapons," I added. "There are three of us besides Forbush. I see the victors have neglected to secure the captured arms on the forward deck. We can jump down, arm ourselves, and fight it out."

"But there are nearly a hundred of the rascals," answered Captain Underwood. "Some of them are pretty well grown, and all of them have been exercised with the bayonet. I don't relish having one of those things stuck into me, and I shouldn't dare to punch any boy with such an ugly iron. I think

I would rather do what fighting I do without any bayonet."

The captain was a very prudent man, certainly; and I was aware how dangerous it would be to injure one of the Wimpletonians. They were reckless; we were cautious, and fearful of hurting them; so that they had every advantage over us, besides that of mere numbers. While we were debating the question, Forbush appeared on the forward deck. One of his hands was covered with blood, and it was plain he had not abandoned his post without an attempt to retain it.

"Captain Underwood, they have driven me out of the engine-room at the point of the bayonet," said the engineer, holding up his bloody hand.

"Come up here," replied the captain.

"We have a good head of steam on, and the engine needs some one to look out for it."

"Go and fix it as it ought to be!" said the imperious Major Waddie, as he stalked up to the engineer with his drawn sword in his hand.

"If there were no one but you on board, I would blow you so high you would never come down again," added Forbush, as he glanced at his wound‚ed hand.

"None of your impudence, but do as I tell you,' puffed Waddie.

"Look out for the engine, Forbush," added the captain; "and speak to the fireman."

Forbush went to the engine, and presently the sound of the steam hissing through the escape pipe assured us the peril of an explosion was provided for. The engineer, having attended to this duty, appeared upon the forward deck again. He was not a very demonstrative man, but I could see that he was nursing his wrath under the imperious manner of Waddie. Passing through the Wimpletonians, he went to the bow of the boat.

"Major, there is Wolf Penniman in the wheelhouse," said Dick Bayard, as he discovered me at one of the windows.

"We'll fix him in due time," replied Waddie, as he glanced up at me with an ugly look, which assured me I had nothing to hope for from his magnanimity. "We must get rid of those fellows in the cabin next."

"Well, what are you going to do with them?" asked Captain Ben Pinkerton.

"Land them in some out-of-the-way place on the east shore, where it will take them all day to get home again," suggested Captain Dick Bayard.

"Where?" inquired Major Waddie, apparently pleased with the idea.

"At the point off the North Shoe, for instance," replied Bayard.

"That's the plan!" exclaimed the major, as he sheathed his glittering blade, apparently satisfied that the battle was finished. "Wolf Penniman, come down here!" he added, turning to me again.

"No, I thank you," I replied, cheerfully.

"If you want to get out of this scrape with a whole skin, you had better mind what I tell you," continued Waddie, involuntarily putting his hand on the hilt of his sword.

"I think I can best keep a whole skin up here," answered.

"Better go down," interposed the captain. "Moses and I will go with you."

Moses was one of the deck hands, who had been

steering when the capture was made. There were two more of them, besides the fireman below, making seven men on board.

"Very well; if you think best I will go down," I replied.

"We had better keep together," he added.

I led the way down the ladder, and as the captain followed me, he beckoned to the deck hands to keep near us.

"You have concluded to mind — have you?" sneered Waddie, as I presented myself before his imperial majorship.

"I concluded to come down," I answered.

"Wolf, you will go to the engine-room, and mind the bells," he continued.

"Mr. Forbush is the engineer of this boat," I replied.

"No matter if he is; you will do as I tell you, or take the consequences."

"Then I will take the consequences," I answered, for I had no intention of helping the Wimpletonians land their conquered foe on the North Point.

"Here! form around him! Charge bayonets!

Drive him into the engine-room!" said Waddie, smartly.

Instead of waiting for this programme to be carried out, I walked forward to the extreme point of the bow, where the engineer had taken position. I was not quite sure that I could successfully resist the order; but it was not in my nature to obey the haughty commands of Major Waddie.

"That's right!" said Forbush, as I joined him. "I'm glad to see a little grit."

Captain Underwood and the three deck hands followed me; but Waddie drew his sword, and, filled with rage, crowded through them towards me.

"Wolf, I command this boat now, and I order you to the engine-room," fumed the major, as he pointed his sword at me, as though he intended to run me through; and I am not sure that such was not his purpose.

Forbush's patience appeared to be exhausted, and before I had time to make any reply, he suddenly sprang upon Waddie, wrenched the sword from his grasp, and, seizing him by the collar, jammed him against the rail with so much force, that the bantam major howled with pain and terror. The dignity of his military position was knocked out of him, and the glory of the chapeau, feathers, and gold lace departed.

"Look out for the rest of them!" called Forbush.

I picked up one of the guns which the captors had thrown one side, and the three deck hands followed my example. Captain Underwood, still true to his humane philosophy, took a handspike. But the sudden movement of the engineer seemed to paralyze the valiant soldiers for the moment, as they paused to see what the grimy Forbush intended to do with their leader.

"Rally! rally!" shouted Captain Bayard, who, now that the major was *hors de combat*, was the ranking officer. "Charge bayonets!"

"You keep back!" replied Forbush. "If one of you takes a single step forward, I will throw this fellow overboard;" and he jammed poor Waddie against the rail again, until we could almost hear his bones crack.

"Don't! don't!" groaned Waddie. "Keep the fellows back, Dick Bayard, or he will kill me!"

"That's so," replied the stout engineer, who did not weigh less than one hundred and eighty, and was six feet high.

By this time the four men and myself were drawn up in line of battle. It was clear enough to the Wimpletonians that, if the action began, there would be some broken heads, if not bleeding bodies. However lightly they regarded bayonet wounds when the weapons were in their own hands only, they seemed to have a great respect for the cold steel in the hands of others. They formed their line in the act of charging bayonets; but they did not charge any. There they stood, arrested by the plaintive cry of their gallant leader.

"Now, come out here, Feathers!" said Forbush, as he took Waddie by the collar, besmearing the major's face with blood from his wounded hand, and trotting him up to the line. "Come up here again, and take command! Order these cubs upon the hurricane deck, or I will make short work of you!"

The engineer emphasized his commands by shaking Waddie most unmercifully.

"You let me alone!" howled the discomfited commander of the battalion.

"I'll let you alone when I have done with you," added Forbush, as he twisted his gripe upon the collar of his victim, so as almost to choke him.

"You'll kill me!" gasped Waddie.

"Will you give the order I told you?"

"Send the fellows upon the hurricane deck!" whined Waddie to Dick Bayard, crying and howling at the same time.

"Don't do it, Dick!" said Pinkerton, who could not endure the thought of having the victory wrested from the conquerors in the very moment of their triumph.

"Waddie says so. What can we do?" replied Bayard.

"They don't mind," added Forbush, shaking the unfortunate major again.

"Do as I tell you, Dick Bayard!" called Waddie, writhing under the torture.

Very reluctantly the senior captain gave the order, and the Wimpletonians crept up the ladders to the hurricane deck.

"Now let me alone!" growled Waddie, trying to shake off his powerful persecutor.

8

"Hold still, Feathers!" replied Forbush, applying a little gentle force, as if to assure his victim that the tragedy was not yet ended.

The engineer was now in excellent humor, and was exceedingly pleased with the turn he had given to the affair.

"Ain't you going to let me go now?" added the major, in a pleading tone.

"Not yet, Feathers. You must give security for the good behavior of your crowd."

"What are you going to do with me?" asked Waddie.

"I'm going to throw you overboard if you don't behave like a man. Now, Captain Underwood, you can let out our boys. These rascals have locked them up in the cabin."

"Better get rid of the Wimps first," I whispered to the captain.

"What shall we do with these fellows?" he replied, with a significant glance at me, as he comprehended my meaning.

"Land them at North Point," I suggested.

"Good!" laughed Forbush. "It is a poor rule

that won't work both ways. What do you say, Captain Underwood?"

"Anything to get rid of them!" replied the captain, impatiently.

"Very well; I will take care of Feathers. I will keep him in the engine-room with me," added Forbush. "Now, Wolf, you and the three deck hands stay here. If those fellows up there attempt anything mischievous, you call me, and Feathers and I will settle it — won't we, Feathers?"

Forbush laughed till his fat sides shook, and then dragged Major Waddie to the engine-room.

CHAPTER X.

KEEPING THE PEACE.

"HADN'T we better let our boys out before we go ahead?" asked Captain Underwood, in a low tone, as the engineer disappeared with his prisoner.

"There will be a fight if we do," I replied. "We can land the Wimps in ten or fifteen minutes."

"What will Tommy say?" added Captain Underwood.

"No matter what he says. It is better to keep the peace than to let them out."

Doubtless he fully agreed with me; but he dreaded the wrath of his employer's son even more than the violence of the Wimpletonians. He went up to the wheel-house, and rang the bell to go ahead. The discomfited enemy on the hurricane deck were discussing the exciting topic very earnestly. It was humiliating for all of them to lay down their arms, practically, on account of the capture of their leader. Ben Pinkerton was in favor of fighting it out, and rescuing Waddie from the gripe of his persecutor by force and arms; but timid counsels finally prevailed, and the battalion kept quiet.

I had gone up the ladder when the boat started, so that I could see what they were doing, and hear what they were saying; but I kept my line of retreat open, so that I could make for the forward deck if a storm appeared. It was only a short run to North Point, and we soon made the landing at a rude pier, erected for passengers going to an interior town. As soon as the steamer was made fast, Forbush appeared on the forward deck, dragging Waddie by the collar, and carrying the sword in his hand. Taking position in the bow of the boat, where he could not be assaulted in the rear, the engineer planted his prisoner in front of him, while the deck hands, reënforced by the fireman and myself, formed a line between him and the gangway.

"Now, Feathers, if your men are good soldiers

they will obey you," Forbush began. "Just give them the order to march down in single file, and go ashore!"

Waddie was humiliated by his defeat. He was ashamed to confess, practically, that the battalion had been defeated by his regard for his own safety. But he was still in the power of the fierce engineer, whose bloody hand was upon his throat. He hesitated; but every instant of delay caused Forbush to tighten his hold, and it was painfully apparent to him that he must give the order, or be choked by his unrelenting tyrant.

"Speak, Feathers, speak!" said the engineer. "Give your orders, and speak up like a man, so that they can hear you!"

"Don't! Don't! You hurt me!" whined the major.

"That's nothing to what will come if you don't do as I tell you."

"March them down, Dick Bayard," howled Waddie, as Forbush emphasized his determination by a fierce twist at the neck of his victim.

"In single file," added the engineer.

" Single file, Dick ! " repeated Waddie.

" Single file — forward, march ! " said Captain Dick Bayard, who was plainly disgusted with the proceedings.

The column of valiant warriors, grand even in their misfortunes, descended the ladder on the port side, and stepped on shore. They looked as sheepish as the lambs on the neighboring hills; but they were full of bottled-up rage, and as soon as Waddie was out of trouble, it was probable that something would be done.

" Now let me go ! " snapped Waddie, when the last of the file had left the boat.

" Not yet, Feathers," replied Forbush, as he glanced at the two companies on the pier. " Order your troops to march up to the grove on the shore."

" What for ? " groaned Waddie.

" Good soldiers never ask questions," laughed the engineer, as he twisted the major's collar again.

Waddie gave the order as he was required, and Dick Bayard, who appeared to be on the watch for a chance to redeem the fortunes of the day, doggedly led the battalion away from the steamer.

"Now it is all right, Feathers," said Forbush. "Next time, when you want a steamer, you had better apply at the captain's office."

"I didn't want your old steamer," snarled the gallant major.

"What did you take her for, then?"

"Because you were going to run down our boats. I heard Tommy Toppleton tell the captain to do so."

"Why didn't you get out of the way?"

"We never get out of the way for Toppleton humbugs," sneered Waddie. "You haven't seen the end of this."

"We shall probably see the end of it together. Here is your cheese knife, Feathers; but behave yourself, or you haven't seen the worst of it yet. Mind that, Feathers!"

Waddie took his sword, and looked daggers; but he dared not use any, or even the weapon he held in his hand. Sullenly, he walked across the deck to the pier. He wanted to do something, but he was prudent when his own person was in peril.

"Cast off the fasts, Moses," said Forbush, as he hastened to the engine-room.

"Come down here!" shouted Major Waddie to his forces in the grove. "Come! Double quick!"

I do not know what the valiant major intended to do next; but probably, if his forces had not been sent to the grove by the forethought of the engineer, he would have ordered an assault upon the Middleport, and endeavored to recapture her. He would have directed his troops to charge upon anything, so long as he could keep behind them, and make good his own escape in case of disaster. He was reckless enough to do anything; but as soon as the fasts were cast off, Captain Underwood rang to back her, and the boat was clear of the pier long before Waddie could bring up his forces.

"We are well out of that," said the captain, as he rang to go ahead. "Now you can let our boys out of the cabin."

I was not exactly satisfied with the situation in which I found myself, for though I was very happy

in having escaped the wrath of Waddie Wimpleton, I had still to encounter the ire of the other
"scion of a noble house." I had expected to be
broiled on a gridiron, or subjected to some fearful
punishment, for my sins against the house of Wimpleton; and probably I should have been a sufferer,
if Forbush had not taken the matter in hand, and
brought it to an issue. Now Tommy would berate
me for refusing to obey his order, when the engineer had declined to do so; but I was willing to
meet this charge, if I could escape the responsibil-
ity of advising the captain to keep "our boys" prisoners after we had subdued the enemy.

I went to the cabin door to discharge my mission.
It had been fastened with a piece of wood, placed
in the staple over the hasp, for the padlock with
which it was usually secured was lost. I threw
the door wide open, and announced to the prisoners below that they were free.

"The door is open, Major Toppleton," called one
of the students to his chief.

"Where are the Wimps?" demanded Major Tommy, as he led the way out of the cabin.

"We put them on shore here, at North Point, where they intended to land you," I replied.

"Why didn't you obey my order when I told you to take charge of the engine?" continued Tommy, his face beginning to kindle up with anger again.

"I couldn't take the engine out of Mr. Forbush's hands," I replied with becoming meekness.

"Forbush shall be discharged when the boat returns," said Tommy, shaking his head.

"Perhaps you will change your mind when you learn what he has done," I suggested. "He recaptured the boat, after he had been driven at the point of the bayonet from the engine-room. He was wounded in the hand, too, in the scrape. I don't know how we should have got out of it if it hadn't been for him. He is a plucky fellow, and stood up against the bayonets of the whole crowd of Wimps."

"What did he do?" asked Tommy, curiously.

"He captured Waddie Wimpleton, took his sword away from him, and made him order his command to the hurricane deck."

"When was that?"

"Well, a short time ago," I replied, cautiously.

"Why didn't you let us out then?" he demanded.

"All the Wimps were here on deck. We let you out just as soon as we got rid of them."

"What did you let them go for, if you had Waddie?"

"There were two companies of them, and they were armed with bayonets. We were glad enough to get rid of them."

Tommy thought, if he had been called with his force, he could have taken care of the Wimpletonians; but he behaved better than I expected. I turned his attention back to Forbush, and minutely described to the major and his men the operations of the engineer, and the conduct of Waddie under the torture. Tommy laughed, and the soldiers laughed. It was a good joke, and they were sorry they had not seen the fun.

"I hope you won't find fault with Mr. Forbush, after the good service he has rendered, and the cut he received in the hand in doing his duty," I ventured to suggest.

"No! No! No!" murmured the boys.

"I am willing to forgive him," replied Tommy, magnanimously. "But if he had obeyed my order, there would have been no trouble."

"What do you think the consequences would have been if he had obeyed your order?" I mildly inquired.

"No matter what they were; both he and you ought to have done as I told you to do."

"The fellows in the boats would have been smashed up under the wheels of the steamer."

"No, they wouldn't. I only meant to duck them a little. I should have stopped the wheels in a minute."

I was very glad to hear Tommy acknowledge that he did not mean to annihilate the Wimpletonians, for I had a very good opinion of him, on the whole. Though he did not mean seriously to injure the enemy, I have no doubt some of them would have been sacrificed if he could have had his own way. It is a blessed thing that boys can't always have their own way.

I walked with Tommy to the engine-room, where Forbush was binding up the wound on his hand.

The little major kindly inquired about the injury, and thanked the engineer for the service he had rendered; but he could not help adding that it would have been better if the order he gave had been obeyed. He then went up to the wheel-house to see the captain; and as it did not appear that he had done anything worthy of especial commendation, Tommy wanted to know why he had not let him out of the cabin sooner.

"We didn't think it was best to open the doors till we had landed the Wimpletonians," replied Captain Underwood, with more candor than prudence.

"You didn't, eh?" said Tommy, waxing angry.

"Wolf thought you wouldn't care to see the other boys."

"Then he advised you not to let us out — did he?"

"He thought it wasn't best; and I thought so too," added the captain, willing to share the blame with me.

"What did you mean, Wolf?" demanded the major, turning to me.

"The Wimps had two companies, and you had only one," I replied; but it was in vain that I tried to smooth the matter over.

He was mad with me, because, in my capacity as a messenger of peace, I had prevented a fight; but I was satisfied. The boat ran up to the landing-place on the Horse Shoe, and the "troops" and their baggage were disembarked.

"Wolf, you may go back to Middleport in the steamer; I don't want you here," said Tommy.

But I was the ambassador of peace!

CHAPTER XI.

AT THE HORSE SHOE.

"I SHOULD like to stay with you a few days, Major Tommy," I ventured to say, after the young lord had given me the imperative order to depart on the steamer.

"I say I don't want you here," replied Tommy, flatly. "We can get along without you."

"Perhaps I may be of some service to you," I modestly suggested.

"I don't want any fellow about me that won't obey orders," protested the little major. "You advised the captain to keep us locked up in that cabin, when we might have cleaned out the Wimps, and paid them off for what they did."

"Your father sent me down here, Tommy, to do anything I could to assist you," I added.

"I don't care if he did!" replied Tommy, irritated rather than conciliated by this remark.

"He wished me to stay with you; it was not by my own desire that I came."

"Did he send you here to be a spy upon our actions? If he did, so much the more reason why we should get rid of you. We don't want any spies and go-betweens here."

"I am not a spy, Tommy."

"Go on board the steamer, and tell my father I won't have you here."

"Very well," I replied, as I walked away from the imperious little magnate.

"Wolf is a good fellow," I heard the dignified Skotchley say to Tommy, as I departed. "I wouldn't send him off."

"You wouldn't, and you needn't. I will, and shall," replied Tommy, curtly.

By this time the officers and soldiers of Company A had gathered at the shore, and I found I had quite a number of friends who were willing to intercede for me; but if all the officers of the battalion had gone down upon their knees to him in my behalf, he would not have yielded. I was banished from the island; and, though I was very will-

9

ing to go, much preferring to spend my vacation in
some contemplated improvements upon our garden,
I did not wish to be sent away in disgrace. I saw
that Skotchley did not like the manner in which
his interposition had been treated, and just as the
boat was about to start, I was not a little surprised
to see him come on board.

"Faxon is as mad as a March hare," said he, walk-
ing up to me.

"What is the matter?"

"He says it is mean to send you off in this way."

"I am willing to go; I don't care about staying
here, for there will be a fight soon," I added. "But
Major Toppleton sent me here, and I thought I
ought to stay."

"I would stay, if I were you," said Skotchley.

"No; I won't make any trouble. But the steamer is starting; you will be carried off if you don't
go on shore."

"That is just what I want," replied the dignified
student, with a smile. "Like yourself, I don't wish
to make any trouble; but I will not be snubbed by
Major Tommy Toppleton. I prefer to spend my
vacation in some other place."

"All ashore," said Captain Underwood, nodding to my companion.

"I am going with you, captain."

"Very well;" and the bell was rung to start her.

"Hallo, there! Stop her, Captain Underwood!" called the imperious major.

The captain obeyed, of course.

"Where are you going, Skotchley?" demanded Tommy.

"I am going to Middleport," replied Skotchley, in his quiet manner.

"I don't see it!" added the major, his face reddening with anger at this breach of discipline. "You are first lieutenant of Company B."

"I prefer not to remain."

"But I prefer that you should remain," stormed Tommy.

"I am sorry to disappoint you, but I have decided to go."

"Will you come on shore, or will you be brought on shore?"

"Neither."

"Captain Briscoe, take a file of men, and bring

Skotchley on shore. He is a deserter," added
Tommy.

Whew! A deserter!

"Go ahead, captain," I suggested to the timid
master of the steamer. "There will be a row here
in five minutes, if you don't."

"It is all my place is worth to disobey that strip-
ling," replied Captain Underwood, disgusted with
the situation. "His father rules all Middleport, and
he rules his father."

I saw Faxon remonstrating in the most vigorous
manner with the commander of the battalion, and
presently the former came on board with the olive
of peace in his hand. He begged Skotchley to return to the shore, in order to save all further
trouble.

"If Tommy will permit Wolf to remain, I will,"
replied the dignified student.

Faxon returned to the shore with these terms;
but Tommy indignantly declined them. He would
have Skotchley, and he would not have me. The
order was given again for Captain Briscoe to bring
the refractory lieutenant on shore with a file of sol-

diers; but the men would not "fall in" to execute such a command. Skotchley was the most influential fellow among the students, as his election to the presidency of the railroad proved. Though he was dignified, and remarkably correct in his deportment, he was very popular. Tommy had just snubbed him, and this had excited the indignation of the crowd. Briscoe and a dozen others threatened to leave the camp, and actually made a movement towards the steamer.

Major Tommy was in a quandary. There was a mutiny among the forces, and the prospect at that moment was the breaking up of the camp. The students had long been disgusted with Tommy's tyranny, and it did not require much to kindle the flames of insurrection in the battalion. Hurried consultations among groups of officers and privates indicated a tempest. The little magnate was shrewd enough now to see that he had gone too far, but his pride would not permit him to recede.

The disaffected ones who had the courage to strike for their own rights were collecting near the pier. Briscoe appeared to be the leading rebel, and the force which gathered around him included half the battalion. Tommy was informed that they intended to desert in a body.

" Start your boat, Captain Underwood," said Tommy, in order to prevent the departure of the rebels.

The captain pulled the bells, and the wheels of the Middleport turned.

"Now stop her!" shouted the major; and it was evident that he intended only to move the steamer far enough from the shore to prevent the escape of the disaffected portion of his command.

I heard the last order, but the captain did not, for I had moved to the stern, in order to see the result.

" Stop her, I say," repeated Tommy, savagely.

Still Captain Underwood did not, or would not, hear him, and the Middleport went on her way.

" Tell the captain to stop her!" screamed Tommy, at the top of his lungs.

I deemed it to be in the interests of peace not to heed this order, for I was afraid, if I communicated it to the captain, he would obey. The little major screamed till he was hoarse; but we were clear of the island, though it was certain there was an account to be settled in the future.

"Our Academy would be a great institution, if Tommy Toppleton went to school somewhere else," said Skotchley.

"It is a great pity he is so overbearing," I replied.

"He seems to think all the rest of the fellows were created only to be his servants, and he treads upon them as though they were worms beneath his feet. I have not been accustomed to have a fellow speak to me as he did to-day."

"He is very haughty; but he is a generous fellow, and has many other good qualities."

"But one can't live with him, he is so overbearing. I am rather sorry now that I did not accept the office of president of the Lake Shore Railroad, when I was elected. It would have brought affairs to a head. But I did not want to spite him, for he never treated me so badly before."

Tommy had made a great mistake in alienating such a fellow as Skotchley. It was evident that the tempest among the students could not much longer be delayed, if it had not already commenced. From the deck of the Middleport, we saw the two companies march to the camp ground, and begin to pitch the tents. It was probable that the mutiny had been nipped in the bud by the departure of the steamer with Skotchley on board. I was afterwards told that the students regarded Tommy's order to start the boat as yielding the point, and that, when he failed to stop her, he accepted the situation, and made a virtue of necessity, permitting the boys to believe that the Middleport had departed in obedience to his command.

The boats of the Wimpletonians were moving towards North Point, for those in charge of them had comprehended the final defeat of their party. It only remained for them to seek another camp ground, or make the attempt to drive the Toppletonians from their position. Skotchley and I agreed that they would not long be quiet, and that the week would be filled up with quarrels and skir, mishes between the students of the rival academies

In an hour the steamer arrived at the wharf in

Middleport, and we went on shore. I invited Skotchley, as the Institute was closed, to spend the week with me at my father's house. He thanked me very cordially, and accepted the invitation; but before I went home, I deemed it proper to report to Major Toppleton the events which had transpired during the forenoon. I intended to call at his house on my way home; but we met him coming down the street towards the pier.

"I thought you went up to the camp, Wolf," said he, much surprised when he saw me.

"I have been, sir, and a sweet time we have had of it. Tommy sent me off, and would not permit me to remain on the island."

"What has happened?" he asked, anxiously.

I told him the story of the morning's adventures, though it took me half an hour to do so.

"And Tommy sent you off—did he?" laughed the major.

"Yes, sir—because I advised the captain not to let our fellows out of the cabin until we got rid of the Wimps; but if they had been let out, there would have been a fight with bayonets."

"I am very glad you didn't let them out then; but Tommy is rather a difficult subject to manage," continued the major, lightly. "I have to coax him a great deal, for he is bound to have his own way. If he is thwarted, it has a bad effect upon him. I sent you up to the island to keep the run of things there; but of course I did not expect you to oppose him."

"I did the best I could, sir."

"You did very well; but I am sorry Tommy sent you away, for I thought you might have some influence with him. Did he send you away too, Skotchley?" he added, turning to my companion.

"No, sir; I came of my own accord," replied the dignified student: but he did not think it necessary to add that he and Tommy had fallen out.

"You think there will be a fight between the two sides up there?" continued the major.

"Before the week is out there will be."

"Something must be done," said the major, anxiously.

I saw now that he was quite as much the victim of Tommy's waywardness as the students of the Institute.

CHAPTER XII.

UP THE LAKE.

MAJOR TOPPLETON was absolutely afraid of his son. There was a rumor in Middleport — though I did not hear of it until after the events narrated had transpired — that his father had positively refused to permit Tommy to have his own way on one occasion, when the young gentleman insisted upon discharging a favorite servant of his mother. The major declined to yield, and stuck to his text. The result was, that Tommy, in his rage, ran away in the dead of winter, and was not found for two whole days, during which time he lived on the fat of the land at the Hitaca House, whither he had gone in the steamer. He refused to go home till his father promised to discharge the obnoxious servant, declaring that he would not live in the same house with the woman, and threatening to go to

New York and ship as a common sailor. Undoubt-
edly it would have been better for the young gentleman if he had shipped as a common sailor, for in
that capacity he would have ascertained how much
of his own way he could enjoy. His father yielded,
and Tommy, having conquered in this instance, had
no trouble in maintaining his supremacy. The major was afraid he would run away, or do some other
terrible thing; and the man who was the lord and
master of all Middleport was the slave of his tyrannical son. This is not the only instance on record of
the same thing.

I supposed Major Toppleton would take some
steps to prevent a quarrel between the rival students,
but he did not. It was a delicate and difficult matter to interfere with Tommy; and the fact that I
had been sent back proved that he would not submit to any dictation, or even suggestion.

"I am rather glad you have come back, Wolf,"
said the great man; and I saw that he was trying
to conceal his anxiety in regard to the students.
"I have just received a letter from Hitaca, informing me that my new yacht is finished, and I was

on my way to the wharf to find some one to send after her. I have been told that you are a boatman as well as an engineer, Wolf."

"I have handled all sorts of boats on the lake. I used to sail the Marian on the other side; and she is the largest boat in this part of the lake," I replied.

"But she is not more than half as large as the Grace."

"The Grace!" I exclaimed, delighted with the name.

"She is called after my daughter. Do you think you can handle her?"

"I know I can, sir."

"She is thirty-five feet long, and measures fifteen tons. She has a cabin large enough to accommodate half a dozen persons."

"I should like to bring her down first rate," I added, glancing at Skotchley; and I saw by his looks that he would like to accompany me.

"If you think you can manage her, you may go. You will want two or three hands to help you."

"I will find them, sir."

"You must take the steamer up the lake as soon as she goes. I will write an order on the builder to deliver the boat to you; call at my house for it before you start."

I was delighted with this mission, for I had a taste for boats almost as strong as that for a steam-engine. I was fond of the water, and should have preferred a situation in a steamer to anything else. Skotchley was as much pleased as I was with the cruise in prospect; and, after I had told my mother where I was going, we called at the major's for the order. He gave me some money to pay the expenses, and, with two of my friends, we embarked in the steamer for Hitaca, where we arrived at half past four. Near the steamer's wharf, up the river, I saw a beautiful yacht, which I at once concluded was the Grace; and she was worthy of her name, if anything made of wood and iron could be equal to such an honor.

I presented my order to the builder, who was in doubt about delivering it to me, whom he stigmatized as a boy; but when I informed him that I was the engineer of the Lake Shore Railroad, he made no further objection. He did me the honor to say that he had heard of me, and that he had ridden in the dummy from Middleport to Spangleport. I was not a little astonished to find that my fame had travelled so far as Hitaca; but it appeared that everybody in the vicinity knew all about the quarrel between the two sides of the lake.

The Grace was moored in a basin of the river, and the builder put my party on board of her in a skiff. She was a magnificent boat, far exceeding anything of the kind I had seen, or even dreamed of. She was sloop-rigged, painted black outside, and white on deck. But her cabin was the principal attraction to me, and I hastened below to inspect it. It was finished and furnished in a style equal to the major's house, with two little state-rooms, and a little cuddy forward, with a cook-stove in it. I was astonished and delighted, and would gladly have resigned my situation as engineer for a position on this beautiful craft.

I sent Tom Walton and Joe Poole up to a store to purchase a list of groceries and provisions which I had made out, with Skotchley's assistance, on board of the steamer; for we should need some supper, and perhaps breakfast, before we could reach Middleport. While they were gone, Skotchley and I devoted ourselves to a new examination of the wonders of the Grace. The builder was pleased with my enthusiasm, and the warm praise both of us bestowed upon his work. He opened all the lockers, and explained everything about the yacht, from the keel to the mast-head.

"When will that railroad be done?" asked the builder, after we had exhausted the Grace, cabin, deck, and rigging.

"In a month or two," I replied; and I could not fail to observe the sly twinkle in his eye.

"They say Major Toppleton has bought up both the steamers, and intends to run them, in connection with the railroad, only from Middleport to Hitaca."

"I have heard so; but I know nothing about it."

"Do you see that steamer?" he added, pointing to a vessel, which had just been launched.

"I see her. Is that the new one Colonel Wimpleton is building?" I asked, with no little curiosity.

"That's the boat, and if I mistake not she will give your road a hard run."

"I should like to see her," I continued.

The builder kindly conducted me all over her. Everything about her was first-class work, and I confess that I rather envied the Wimpletonians the possession of such a steamer. They were just building her cabins and upper works, and I saw that she was to be far ahead of anything on the lake.

"I suppose there will be some lively competition when this boat is finished," said I, as we left the steamer. "But I hope it will be good-natured."

"The boat has rather the advantage of you," added the builder. "If the major will build a bridge over the river at Ucayga, he will win the day. As it is, the steamer will have the weather-gage."

It was hardly prudent for me to think so, for I was to run the "Lightning Express" in opposition to the new boat. But our provisions had arrived, and just then I was more interested in the cruise of the Grace than in the trips of the new steamer. Skotchley and I went on board. As the river below

10

Hitaca was narrow, and the navigation difficult, the builder, with some of his men, assisted us to work her out into the open lake. The wind was tolerably fresh from the westward, and as soon as the men had left us, I took the helm, and headed the Grace for Middleport. The yacht was a furious sailer, and she tore through the water at a rapid rate.

"I rather like this," said Skotchley, as he seated himself at my side.

"So do I," I replied. "I wish the major would make me skipper of this boat, and let some one else run the locomotive."

"I don't want anything better than this for my vacation. I should like to spend the week in her, cruising up and down the lake."

"Perhaps you can. The major is going a fishing in her, I heard him say. Very likely he will let you have a berth in her."

"I'm afraid not. Tommy will spoil all my chances of anything good for this term," added the dignified student, shaking his head.

"I think the fellows on the Horse Shoe are likely

to bring Tommy to his senses before they get through with him. They have him there alone, and I don't think they will let him have his own way all the time. At any rate, they began as though they would not."

"If I were in Tommy's boots, I should try to make the fellows love instead of hate me. He is smart, and can make himself very agreeable when he isn't ugly. In my opinion, there will be a big row on the Horse Shoe, even without any help from the Wimps. Tommy is plucky, and I am not sure that it will not be a good thing for him if the Wimps attack his camp. His position is a little like that of some king I have read of, who got up a foreign war to save himself from being tipped off the throne by his own subjects."

"Supper is ready," said Tom Walton, who attended to the culinary department of the Grace, having had some experience in the art of cooking. "Shall I take the helm, while you go down?"

I was very happy to have him do so, for Tom was a good boatman, which was the particular reason why I had invited him to be one of the party. We

went down into the cabin, where the table was set
for us.   It was neatly and tastily arranged.   The
viands consisted of beefsteak, potatoes, milk toast,
and coffee; and I must do Tom the justice to say
that they tasted as good as they looked.   Certainly
I never felt happier than when I sat down to that
supper.   There was something decidedly marine in
the surroundings.   The fresh breeze created quite a
sea for an inland lake, and the Grace tossed up and
down just enough to make her seem like a vessel.

"Wolf! Wolf!" shouted Tom Walton, at the
helm, just as I was taking my second cup of coffee;
for I did not expect to sleep much that night.

"What's the matter?" I demanded, springing into
the standing-room, fearful that some calamity impended over the beautiful yacht.

"There's some one calling to us from over there,"
he replied, highly excited, as he pointed towards
the eastern shore.   "There he is!   It's a man in a
boat, or on a raft."

"Help! Help!" cried the person, in a voice
which sounded strangely familiar to me.

"Let out the main sheet, Tom. We will run over

and see what the matter is," I replied, taking the helm.

In a few moments the Grace swept round into the wind, under the lee of the person who had appealed to us for aid. He was on a kind of raft, sitting upon the wet planks, over which the waves flowed freely. I ran the bow of the yacht up to his frail craft, to which the sufferer was clinging with both hands. Giving the helm to Tom, I rushed forward to help the man, whose face presented a most woe-begone aspect.

My astonishment may be surmised when I recognized in this person Colonel Wimpleton!

CHAPTER XIII.

IF THINE ENEMY HUNGER.

A S soon as the Grace came within reach of
Colonel Wimpleton, on the raft, he improved
his opportunity. Grasping the bob-stay, he made
his way on board, with my assistance. He was
so clumsy and terrified that without my help he
would certainly have fallen overboard. He plumped
upon the deck on all fours, in a most undignified
attitude for the magnate of Centreport. I helped
him to rise. In doing so, I discovered that his
breath was very odorous of liquor, which seemed
to do something towards explaining the unfortunate plight in which we had found him. He was
not intoxicated at the time he was pulled on board
the Grace; but perhaps he had had time to work
off the effects of the potions whose incense still
lingered about him.

"Wolf Penniman!" exclaimed he, as he grasped one of the fore-stays, and, steadying himself with it, gazed into my face; and his expression seemed to indicate that he would rather have been rescued by any other person than by me.

"Colonel Wimpleton!" I replied, returning his compliment.

"Is it you, Wolf?" he added, as if unwilling to believe the evidence of his own eyes.

"Yes, sir; it is I. But if you feel bad about it, you can return to the raft."

He glanced at the little staging of three planks on which he had made his involuntary cruise, and shuddered as he did so, partly with cold, and partly with dread.

"I will pay you well for whatever you do for me, Wolf," said he, glancing doubtfully at the boat, and then at me.

"Let me tell you in the beginning, Colonel Wimpleton, that you can't pay me the first red cent," I replied, with proper spirit.

"You won't turn me adrift again — will you?"

"No, sir; I will do anything I can for you."

"We have not been very good friends lately."

"No, sir; but that shall not prevent me from assisting you to any extent within my power. What shall I do for you, sir?"

"I am very cold and numb," said he, curling up with the chills that swept through his frame.

"Come into the cabin, sir. I think we can warm and dry you so that you will be quite comfortable."

"Thank you, Wolf;" and I think this was the first time he had ever used a gracious word to me.

Tom Walton had put the helm up, and the yacht filled away on her course again. I took Colonel Wimpleton's arm, and conducted him to the cabin. The fire was still burning in the little cook-room, and shutting down the hatch on the deck, I soon made the place so hot that it almost melted me. Seating my distinguished guest before the stove, I gave him a mug of hot coffee, though, before he drank it, he asked me if there was any brandy on board. I told him we had none, and he contented himself with the coffee, which was quite as beneficial.

Under my mild treatment, the patient gradually recovered the use of his limbs. I went on deck, and sent Tom down to give him some supper; and our zealous cook provided him a fresh beefsteak, coffee, and toast, which Tom said he ate just as though he had been a common man. It was now quite dark, and we were off Southport, on the east shore. The wind had subsided, and we were not likely to reach Middleport before morning. I gave Tom the helm again, and went below to inquire into the colonel's condition. He was still wet, and was fearful that his exposure would bring on the rheumatic fever, to which he was liable. I suggested to him that he should go to bed, and have his clothes dried. For such a man as he was, he was very pliable and lamb-like.

I conducted him to one of the little state-rooms, which contained a wide berth. I put all the blankets on board upon the bed, and the colonel, taking off all his clothes, buried himself in them. I tucked him up, and he declared that he felt quite comfortable. Hanging up all his garments in the cook-room, I filled the stove with wood, assured they would soon dry in the intense heat of the apartment.

"Can I do anything more for you, colonel?" I asked, returning to his room.

"No, thank you, Wolf; I am very comfortable now," he replied from the mass of blankets and quilts which covered him.

"Where do you wish to go, sir?"

"Home! Home!" he answered with energy.

"We are bound for Middleport, sir, and we will land you as soon as we arrive."

"Thank you, Wolf. I feel like a new man now. I was sure I should be drowned. I had been on that raft over three hours."

"Indeed, sir! It was a very uncomfortable craft."

"The lake was very rough, and the waves washed over me every minute. I gave myself up for lost. I suffered all that a man could endure in those three hours," said he, shuddering as he thought of his unpleasant voyage.

Probably, accustomed as he was to luxury and ease, he had had a hard time of it; but a man inured to work and weather would not have suffered half so much as he did; though, chilled and terrified as he was, I did wonder that he had not been washed from his raft, to perish in the deep waters beneath him.

"I am very glad we happened to come along as we did," I added.

"It was fortunate for me, Wolf. I will give you a thousand dollars for the service you have rendered me as soon as I get home."

"Excuse me, sir; but I cannot take anything," I replied, warmly.

"Why not, Wolf?"

"Because I should despise myself if I took anything. There are some things in this world that cannot be paid for with money."

"You are a strange boy, Wolf."

"Perhaps I am; but I think too much of myself to take money for doing a kindness to any one in distress."

"Very likely I can do something else for you."

"I don't require anything to be done for me, Colonel Wimpleton," I persisted.

"If you have been up to Hitaca, probably you have seen the steamer I am building there."

"Yes, sir, I saw her; and a very fine boat she will be."

"I shall want an engineer for her," he suggested.

"Of course you will, sir. An engineer is a necessity in a steamer," I replied; but I refused to bite at the bait he threw out to me.

"Are you the captain of this boat, Wolf?" he asked, glancing round at the pleasant little stateroom in which he was lying.

"For the present I am."

"Whose boat is it?"

"Major Toppleton's."

"I saw her at the yard in Hitaca; but I had no idea she was so large and fine, as she lay in the river."

"She is just finished, and the major sent me up to bring her down to Middleport. I don't suppose I shall go in her again, for I belong on the railroad."

"I know you do," he replied; and his tone seemed to indicate that, at that moment, he was sorry I did.

I did not care to discuss the relations of the two sides of the lake with him, and I turned his attention from the subject by asking what I could do for him.

"I do not need anything more, Wolf. I am warm and comfortable, and I am very much obliged to you for what you have done. Did you know who it was when you saw me on the raft?"

"Yes, sir; I recognized you when the boat came up to the raft."

"You did?"

"Yes, sir; certainly I did."

"Were you not tempted to let me remain where I was?" he asked, raising his head on the bed, so as to see my face.

"No, sir, I was not."

"I should think you would have been."

"Why, I am not a heathen, Colonel Wimpleton!" I replied.

"No; we have had considerable trouble, and I suppose you have no reason to think very kindly of me," stammered he, as though the words almost choked him.

"I don't think you used me just right, sir; but I'm not an Indian."

"I think I should have perished in half an hour more. It was getting dark, and I was as numb as though I had been frozen. But I shall make it all right somehow, Wolf."

"It is all right now."

"Did you see anything of Dr. Pomford as you came up the lake?"

"Dr. Pomford? I don't know him, sir."

"I suppose not. He is from Philadelphia, and is spending a week with me. He is fond of fishing, and we came up here to try our luck."

"But how came you on that raft, sir?" I inquired. "Did you lose your friend overboard?"

"No; we had a boat, which we fastened to the raft on the fishing-ground. We found the raft there, moored with stakes in the deep water. Dr. Pomford had the misfortune to drop his bottle of brandy overboard, after we had been fishing about an hour. Being quite chilly, he went back to the hotel after some more, leaving me on the raft, for the fish were biting well, and I did not like to leave them; besides, he is a younger man than I am, and can move about easier. His boat was fastened to one of the stakes, and I think, when he started, he must have pulled it up. I don't know how it happened, but as soon as the doctor was out of sight behind the cliff, I found myself adrift."

It was not polite for me to say anything; but I could not help thinking, that if the brandy bottle had dropped overboard sooner, the colonel would have understood the matter better. I had never heard that the great man was in the habit of drinking too much; but the odor of his breath led me to my conclusion. I think he was somewhat fuddled, or he would have gone with the doctor in the boat.

"I never suffered so much in three hours before in my life," continued the colonel. "No canal boat, steamer, or other craft came near me, and I cried for help till my voice gave out. Wolf, I would have given half my fortune, if not the whole of it, to have been taken from that raft a moment before you saw me. If I had known you were in charge of the boat, I should not have expected you to save me."

"My mother always taught me to love my enemies," I answered.

"I hear the ministers talk about such things, but I never believed much in them. I am under very great obligations to you, Wolf. You have treated me as well as though I had always been your best friend."

"It is all right, sir. I am satisfied, if you are."

"I am not satisfied; and I shall never be satisfied until I have made you some return for all this."

"I shall not take anything, sir," I replied, resolutely.

"I will give you a man's wages, if you will take the place as engineer of the new steamer."

"Thank you for the offer, Colonel Wimpleton; but I cannot accept it at present. I never desert my friends till they kick me."

"That is as much as to say that I kicked you before you left Centreport."

"I think we had better bury the past."

"I will make it all right with your father; he shall have better wages than he has now."

"I am much obliged to you, sir; but we are both of us very well satisfied where we are."

The great man seemed to be intensely annoyed at my obstinacy; and it certainly was a hard case for him that he was not permitted even to do me a favor. My pride would not permit me to accept a gift from one who had treated me so badly as he had; but it was a pleasure to serve him, to heap the fiery coals of kindness upon his head.

As I had feared, the wind died out entirely, and the Grace lay helpless upon the smooth surface of the lake. But below, everything was cheerful — even Colonel Wimpleton. The lamps burned brightly in the cabin and state-room, and I enjoyed myself hugely, not caring whether the wind blew or not. I gave the great man his underclothing when it was dry, and he put it on. He wanted to talk, and he did talk in his bed till nearly midnight, when a breeze from the southward sprang up, which compelled me to take my place at the helm. The wind freshened, and the Grace flew before it, so that we came to anchor at two o'clock off Major Toppleton's mansion.

11

CHAPTER XIV.

COLONEL WIMPLETON BIDS HIGH.

DURING the run of twenty miles down the lake, I had sat alone at the helm the greater portion of the time, for my companions were disposed to sleep. Colonel Wimpleton snored so that I could hear him in the standing-room. Skotchley had turned in, occupying the port state-room, while Tom Walton lay on a locker, where I could call him in a moment if his services were needed. While I sat there I did a great deal of heavy thinking, mostly over the relations of Toppleton and Wimpleton. When that magnificent steamer was completed, there would be lively times on the lake.

The offer which Colonel Wimpleton had made me of the position of engineer on board the new steamer was very tempting to me, and I wished very much that I could honorably accept it; but it was no use to think about it. Whatever might be said of Major Tommy, his father had invariably treated me very handsomely. He had come to my father's assistance at a time when he needed help, and had actually put over two thousand dollars into his pocket. I felt it to be my duty to endure a great deal from the son for the sake of the father, as, it now appeared, the former was the chief man of the two.

As we approached Middleport, I called Tom Walton, and, with as little noise as ·possible, anchored the Grace. It was a moonlight night, and since the wind had come up from the southward, the weather was warm and pleasant. The sleepers below had not been disturbed; but, after Tom and I had made everything snug on deck, I waked Colonel Wimpleton, and told him where we were. I offered to row him across the lake in the little tender of the Grace.

"Thank you, Wolf. I will get up at once," said he. "What time is it?"

"About half past two, sir?"

"I have slept well. I had no idea of getting home to-night."

"We are at anchor off Major Toppleton's house."

"Then I think I had better leave as soon as possible. I hope the major won't punish you for what you have done for me."

"I don't think he will. We get along very well together, sir."

"Better than you did with me, I suppose," replied he, with a grim smile. "But I never knew you before, Wolf. It would be different if you should come over to Centreport again."

"I will have the boat ready in a few moments," I replied, wishing to change the subject.

I carried the colonel's clothing to him. It had been nicely dried, and in a few moments he appeared on deck. I could hardly believe he was the Colonel Wimpleton who had been so unjust, not to say savage, towards me. He was a lamb now, and I was very willing to believe that his three hours of peril had done him a great deal of good, though I was afraid the impression would be removed when he returned to his usual associations. I helped the great man into the boat, and pushed off.

"Have you thought of the offer that I made

you, Wolf?" said the colonel, as I gave way at the oars.

"It is useless for me to think of it, sir. I cannot leave Major Toppleton while he wishes me to stay with him."

"But I offer you double your present wages."

"The major has been very kind to me, and was a good friend to our family when we needed a friend. It would not be right for me to leave him, and I cannot think of such a thing."

The magnate of Centreport seemed to me to be more nettled by my refusal than I thought the occasion required. But I enjoyed a certain triumph in finding him thus teasing me to return to his side of the lake — a triumph which was none the less grateful because I had won it by kindness. The colonel was silent for a few moments, hitching about in the boat as though the seat was not comfortable.

"How old are you, Wolf?" he asked, with sudden energy.

"Sixteen in July, sir."

"I have one more offer to make you," he added.

"It won't do any good, Colonel Wimpleton; for,

as I have said, I never desert my friends while they use me well. If you would fill this boat up with gold, it wouldn't make any difference with me," I replied, rather warmly.

"Don't be obstinate, Wolf."

"I am very much obliged to you, sir, for your kind offer, and I would accept it if I could."

"You shall be captain of the new steamer, and have two dollars a day for your services. You will have a nice state-room in the boat, and nothing to do but superintend the management of her. I find you are very popular, not with the boys alone, but with the men and women, and it is for my interest to have you on the steamer."

"I thank you very much, sir; but I cannot leave my present place."

"Think of it, Wolf; and talk the matter over with your father. If you like, he shall be the engineer of the steamer."

"I thought the boat was to be managed by boys."

"But I can't trust every boy in the engine-room. If I can't get you as engineer, I must have a man."

"I should be very glad to take either of the

places you offer me, but I cannot, sir. Major Toppleton has done the handsome thing for me and for my father, and I think you would despise me if I turned against him."

He continued to press the matter with so much earnestness that I came to think I was of a great deal more importance in the world than I really was. But I was steadfast in my allegiance to the friend who had served our family when we were in distress. I pulled the boat up to the steps in front of the colonel's house, and assisted him to get out. He invited me to go in with him, but I declined.

"Now, Wolf, I'm not going to let this affair pass off without doing something for you. I feel that you have saved my life," said he, as I seated myself at the oars.

"It's all right as it is, sir."

"No, it isn't. You will hear from me again soon."

I gave way at the oars, and he walked towards his house. I had conquered him, and it was certainly very remarkable that I had, at this moment, both the mighty men as my friends, though my relations with Tommy Toppleton threatened to make

a breach with one of them. I felt that I had carried out the spirit of my mother's instructions, and
I ought not to be blamed for thinking very kindly
of myself, because I had discharged my Christian
duty to one who had taught me to be his enemy.
In this frame of mind I pulled back to the Grace,
and leaped upon deck.

"What have you been doing, Wolf?" demanded a
stern voice, as a tall form emerged from the cabin.

Whew! It was Major Toppleton! I could not
imagine what had brought him out of his bed at
that unseasonable hour; and I was speechless with
astonishment.

"What have you been doing, Wolf?" repeated he;
and I saw that all hands had been called.

"I have just landed Colonel Wimpleton at his
house, sir," I replied, with due deference.

"And you have been entertaining my greatest
enemy in my yacht — have you?" added the major,
in a tone which seemed to threaten the pleasant
relations that had thus far subsisted between us.

"I picked him up on the lake, when he was per-
ishing with the cold, and in danger of being drowned."

"I don't object to your picking him up when he needed help. One must do that for a dog. But why didn't you put him ashore at the nearest land —in the woods or on the rocks?"

"Because he was so benumbed with cold that he was nearly helpless."

"You gave him a supper at my expense; you could not have used me any better in my own yacht than you did him."

"I did everything I could for him, sir," I replied, humbly.

"You did — did you? Didn't you know that he is a scoundrel? that he is my bitterest enemy?" demanded the major, warmly.

"I did, sir; but I thought it my duty to take care of him when he was suffering."

"Fiddledy-dee! What do you mean by talking such bosh as that to me? I believe you have a soft place in your head, Wolf. Joe Poole says you treated him like a lord. I don't keep a yacht for the accommodation of Wimpleton. If you mean to sell out to the other side, do so at once."

"I have no such intention;" and I was on the

point of defending myself by saying that the colonel had made me several handsome offers, which I had declined; but I concluded such a defence would do me no good, and only irritate the major.

"Of course I should not expect you to let even Wimpleton drown; but you have overdone the thing; you ought to have put him ashore at Southport, or Port Gunga."

"He wanted to come home, sir."

"No matter if he did; I don't keep a yacht for his use."

"I am sorry I have offended you, sir," I added; but I could not regret what I had done.

"Don't do it again. The less you do for the other side, the better you will suit me," he continued, more gently, evidently because his anger had expended itself, rather than because he accepted my apology. How did you get along with the boat?"

"First rate, sir."

"Wolf, I have been uneasy all night about those boys on the island. I have been afraid the Wimpleton scoundrels would tear up the railroad track, and I have kept the dummy going every hour since dark.

I am tired out. I am afraid they will have a fight up at the Horse Shoe, and somebody will get killed. I'm going to bed now; but I want you to run up there, and have an eye upon the boys. You need not go very near the island, but be sure you know what the students are about. The Wimpleton boys have camped on the Shooter, and the two sides are not more than forty rods apart. If things go wrong there, you will run over to Grass Springs, and send me word by Lewis Holgate."

Having delivered his instructions, Joe Poole landed the major before his house. With the assistance of Skotchley and Tom Walton, I hoisted the mainsail and got up the anchor. When Joe returned, both of my companions "pitched into" him for telling the major that I had treated his enemy "like a lord."

"I only told the truth," replied Joe. "But I didn't mean to do Wolf any harm."

"Didn't you know any better?" added Tom.

"I thought I was doing a good thing for Wolf, when I said that he had treated the colonel so well, after he had used him so shabbily."

" Humph, you are a Sunday school scholar ! " sneered Tom.

" So am I, Tom," I interposed. " I don't blame Joe for telling only the truth, and I should have told the major myself if he had not."

This remark quieted the sneerer, and I think that Sunday school doctrine had the better of the argument. Tom run up the jib, and, passing through the Narrows, I headed the Grace for the Horse Shoe. Tom had slept three or four hours, while I had not yet closed my eyes. I gave him the helm, and directing him to call me when we came up with the islands, I stretched myself on the cushioned locker, and dropped asleep.

The day was dawning when the helmsman called me. I had not slept more than an hour and a half; but my interest in the mission upon which I had been sent thoroughly roused me. I took the helm, and going to the eastward of the South Shoe, I headed the Grace through the narrow channel between the Horse Shoe and the Shooter, which would enable me to obtain a fair view of both camps. Major Toppleton's fears were not groundless, for I found that the Wimpletonians had not devoted the night to sleep, as the Toppletonians evidently had, for the former had just effected a landing on the northern part of the Horse Shoe. As the Grace passed out of the channel, I saw the bateaux, loaded with tents and baggage, landing their freight.

A battle impended.

CHAPTER XV.

THE IMPENDING BATTLE.

I CERTAINLY did not expect to find anything at the Horse Shoe or in its vicinity, so early in the morning, to indicate a battle, or even a change of position. Men engaged in a holy cause, or in realizing the promptings of ambition, may fight all day on the bloody field, and then look out for the chances of another day during the darkness of the night; but boys do not do so, as a general rule. The Wimpletonians had evidently done something besides sleeping during the night. Dissatisfied with the proceedings of the first day, they were determined to make a better show the second day.

On the other hand, the Toppletonians appeared to be fast asleep, without even a guard to protect or warn them of the approach of their enemy.

Before daylight the Centreport battalion had been transported from the Shooter to the Horse Shoe, and were now in position to give battle to their haughty foe — if either was more haughty than the other. . I saw them on the shore, landing the last of their baggage, and securing their boats in a little cove. On the highest part of the island I could distinguish, in the gloom of the early morning, a line of sentinels stretching entirely across the land.

Before the Grace was clear of the island, Skotchley, who had made a good night's rest of it, came on deck, and I pointed out to him the change which the Wimpletonians had made.

"What do you think of it, Skotchley?" I asked.

"I think there will be an awful row before noon," he replied, shaking his head. "Of course the Wimps haven't gone over there for nothing."

"I don't know but it would be the best thing in the world to let them fight it out. If one side or the other should get thoroughly thrashed, perhaps both would be willing to keep the peace."

"I think not; for of course the vanquished

party would never be satisfied till it had retrieved its fortunes."

"When do you think the fight will commence?"

"I should say it is liable to begin at any moment," added Skotchley; "but I shall not expect it for several hours after our fellows find out that their territory has been invaded."

"Can we do anything to prevent the fight?" I asked, earnestly.

"I do not see that we can," answered Skotchley. "What can we do? You know what Tommy is. If we should attempt to reason with him, he would flare up."

"I don't mean to reason with him; that would be stupid."

"Of course we can't do anything with Waddie."

"All we have to do is to inform Major Toppleton of the state of affairs on the island," I replied, as I put the helm down, and told Tom Walton to haul in the sheets till the yacht was close on the wind. "We shall get to Middleport with this breeze before the dummy starts."

It was only four o'clock in the morning, and

though we had to beat up to our destination, I was confident the Grace would do it in a couple of hours. I had not had quite rest enough to make me feel good, and giving the helm to Tom, I lay down again. I was soon asleep, and the two hours of rest which I obtained set me right.

"Middleport ahoy!" shouted Tom, as we approached our destination.

"What time is it, Tom?"

"Six o'clock. This yacht makes quick time of it."

"Where is Joe Poole?"

"He has just turned out, and is getting breakfast."

"That's sensible," I replied, going on deck. "Clear away the anchor, and stand by the jib-halyards."

In a few moments more, the Grace was at anchor in the deep water off the major's house. The great man was still asleep; but it would be necessary to wake him. The belligerents on the island would soon be punching each other with their bayonets if something was not done. But I could not help feeling that the presence of Major Toppleton at the scene of action would hardly better

12

the situation. He was as violent, arbitrary, and exacting as his son. It was possible that he might do something to give the victory to the partisans of his own side; but it was hardly to be expected that he would prevent the fight.

"Skotchley, will you go ashore and call upon the major? You have only to tell him that the Wimps have landed on the Horse Shoe," said I to the dignified student.

"I don't object; but why don't you go?" he replied.

"I wish to go somewhere else."

"Where?" he asked, curiously.

"I will tell you some other time, perhaps."

"Just as you like, Wolf."

I pulled up the tender, and both of us got into it. I rowed to the steps in front of the major's house, and landed Skotchley. I had made up my mind what to do, and I had but little time to carry out my purpose. I felt in duty bound to prevent the fight on the island, if I could, even independently of the mighty will and pleasure of Major Toppleton. It was wicked to permit those

boys, armed with deadly weapons, and irritated by
a long-standing rivalry, to plunge into a strife which
might become more serious than either party intended.

"Mr. Wolf!" called the sweet voice of Grace
Toppleton, just as I was about to push off the boat.

I was sorry to meet even her at such a moment,
great as the luxury would have been on an ordinary occasion. She tripped lightly down the walk
to the landing-steps; and certainly she never looked
prettier and more graceful than on that pleasant
summer morning, with the fresh dew, as it were,
glowing upon her cheeks.

"Good morning, Mr. Wolf," she continued, as, out
of breath with the haste she had made, she presented herself before me. "That beautiful yacht!"
she exclaimed, as she glanced at the elegant craft
which bore her name. "Isn't she a sylph!"

"She is all she seems to be," I replied, with becoming enthusiasm, "and I think she is worthy of
her name."

"How very gallant you are, Mr. Wolf!" she
pouted.

"I have been sailing her all night, and I ought to speak well of her."

"Father said he had sent you to Hitaca after her; but we did not expect to see you till this afternoon. I want to go on board of her. I was so surprised when I first saw her this morning!"

It was very awkward, but I could not help myself. I had a mission to perform which must be done at once, or not at all. I could not disregard her wishes, and I assisted her into the boat.

"I have been up to the Horse Shoe, where the students are encamped, since I returned from Hitaca," I continued, as I seated myself at the oars.

"I suppose they are having a nice time up there," she replied.

"I'm afraid not;" and as briefly as I could, I told her the situation of affairs between the contending forces.

As I hoped and expected of one of her gentle nature, she was shocked and alarmed at the prospect of a fight, especially as her brother was foremost in the strife.

"Skotchley has gone up to call your father, and I suppose he will interfere," I added.

"I hope he will;" but the manner in which she spoke seemed to indicate that she entertained the same doubt which had disturbed my calculation.

"I was thinking of doing something more," I replied, rather doubtfully.

"What, Mr. Wolf?"

I related to her my adventure with Colonel Wimpleton during the night, and assured her that the great man of Centreport was very thankful to me for the service I had rendered him.

"I was going over to see him," I added.

"To see Colonel Wimpleton!" she exclaimed, as though she thought such a step would be the sum of all abominations, for even she could not wholly escape the pestilent rivalry that existed between the two sides.

"I am not afraid of him. If I can induce him to compel the students from his side to leave the Horse Shoe, the fight will be avoided."

"I am sorry you said anything to me about it, for father will not let you speak to Colonel Wimpleton about the matter. But, Mr. Wolf, you do as you think best, and I will not say a word."

I assisted her on board of the yacht, and Tom Walton was as polite to her as her beauty and her position required. I was sorry to leave her; but I was intent upon the duty of preventing the fight. I pulled over to the other side of the lake. Haughty servants told me the magnate of Centreport was asleep, and must not be disturbed; but one who had seen me there in the night with the colonel, ventured to tell him that I wished to see him. I was promptly admitted to his bedroom, where I stated my business.

"I don't think there is any great danger of a quarrel," said he, after he had listened attentively to my story.

"I think there is, sir. The students from this side have landed on the Horse Shoe."

"Well, our boys have always used that island for their camp."

"But the Toppleton students engaged the Horse Shoe of the owner, and you will agree with me that they have the best right to the ground. If you will direct the boys from this side to leave the island, there will be no further trouble."

"Do you think I shall tell our boys to run away from those on the other side?" demanded he, indignantly. "I am willing to do anything for you, Wolf, after what has happened; but I think you need not concern yourself about this affair."

"I don't want to have a fight, sir."

"Nor I either."

"Then I hope you will do the right thing, and send your boys off the island."

"I will not do it."

"Well, sir, suppose Waddie should get punched with a bayonet?" I suggested.

"I think Waddie can take care of himself. But, understand me, Wolf, if I can do anything for you, I will do it."

"I have nothing to ask but this."

"I will see what can be done," he replied, rubbing his head, which I judged was still suffering from the effects of the brandy from the bottle that had been lost overboard. "I don't want any fighting. I will go up to the Horse Shoe by and by, if I feel able."

I pressed the matter as strongly as I could; but

the stupid rivalry was too strong in his mind to permit anything which looked like yielding. I left him, hoping that the peril of Waddie, if no higher consideration, might induce him to take some active steps to avert the disgraceful alternative. I pulled with all my might across the lake, and I was not a moment too soon, for I had hardly jumped upon deck before Major Toppleton appeared on the shore, and hailed the yacht for a boat. Taking Grace with me, I pulled to the steps. The great man had his overcoat on his arm, and it was evident that he intended to be a passenger in the yacht to the scene of action.

"Let me go too, father," said Grace. "I must sail in that beautiful yacht this very day."

"We cannot wait," replied the major, rather petulantly.

"I don't want you to wait. I am all ready," she added.

"If there is going to be a fight up there, you will be in the way."

"I will stay in the yacht. Don't say no; be a good papa."

And he was a good papa. Miss Grace was permitted to have her own way, though, being like her mother, who was a very amiable and gentle lady, having her own way did not seem to injure her, as it did her brother. I need not say that I was delighted with the arrangement. We got up the anchor, hoisted the jib, and in a few moments were standing down the lake before the fresh breeze. On the way Joe Poole served up breakfast in good style, and even the major declared that the beefsteak and fried potatoes were excellent.

"The row has commenced!" shouted Tom Walton, at the helm, while we were at the table.

Fortunately our appetites had been satisfied before this startling announcement was made, and we all hastened on deck to see the fight.

CHAPTER XVI.

THE BATTLE OF THE HORSE SHOE.

MISS GRACE TOPPLETON turned pale when Tom announced that the battle had commenced; but her father only uttered an exclamation of rage and impatience. The yacht was just entering the narrow channel between the Horse Shoe and the Shooter, and our position commanded a full view of the field. The Wimpletonians had landed on the north side of the island, near the middle of which was a ridge. The camp of the Toppletonians was at the head of the little bay between the two arms of the Horse Shoe. Behind it was a gentle slope of ground, which terminated at the ridge, beyond which the descent on the north shore was more abrupt.

On this longer declivity, the two hostile battalions were drawn up in the order of battle. The statement that the conflict had commenced was premature; for, though the two "serried ranks" faced each other, no bones had yet been broken. The field presented the traditional aspect of boy fights when the contestants meet in force; the parties faced each other, and each waited for the other to advance. Though I was not an impartial judge, I could not help seeing that the Wimpletonians had displayed more generalship than the Toppletonians; for, instead of waiting on the steeper descent at the north shore, with the ridge above them, for an attack, they had boldly mounted the hill, and taken possession of the high ground, which gave them an advantage that more than compensated for their inferior numbers.

The Toppletonians had not discovered the movement of the enemy till they appeared upon the ridge, which is another convincing proof that "eternal vigilance is the price of liberty." If they had kept even half a dozen sentinels in the exposed portions of the island during the night, they could easily have prevented the landing of the Wimpletonians; but probably they had no suspicion of a night movement.

The combatants appeared to be waiting "for something to turn up;" for, while the Grace was running down the channel and coming to anchor, no movement was made by either of them. The array did not at present indicate the bloody encounter I had feared, and had labored to prevent; but it was plain enough that something would result from the situation. They would not be likely to face each other all day without doing some mischief. I could see Waddie Wimpleton, in his chapeau, white plume, and gold lace, promenading up and down his lines; and, though I could not hear him, I knew very well what big things he was saying.

"Well, what's to be done?" said Major Toppleton, when the Grace had come to anchor.

"If I were you, sir, I would tell our boys to go back into their camp," I replied.

"What! and let the Wimpleton students have it all their own way! Not if I know myself," added the major, indignant even at the suggestion. "Our boys have hired the island, and it belongs to them. They shall stay there!"

The major was as crazy as the colonel had been,

and as neither was willing to sacrifice anything, I could not see how the fight was to be avoided. Of course none of us had any influence with the invaders, and we could not induce them to retire from the island.

"Can't you think of any way to get the Wimpleton boys off, Wolf?" asked the major, impatiently; and I saw that my services were not required as a peacemaker, but rather as an active belligerent.

"I don't see any way now, sir," I replied; "but I may think of something by and by."

"By and by! They may kill each other before you make up your mind," sneered the great man. "I will go on shore."

I pulled up the boat for him, and rowed him to the landing-place. I walked up the slope with him, in order to obtain a better view of the situation. It had already occurred to me that a diversion in the rear of the Wimpletonians might compel them to retire; but, as I was somewhat fearful that such a step would make them more desperate, and hasten the conflict, I did not deem it prudent to suggest the idea. We were within a few rods of the Toppleton line, when Major Tommy discovered us. Whether he was ashamed of his inaction, or fearful that his father would interfere with the pastime he had laid out, I do not know; but our coming evidently had some influence upon him, for he immediately commenced yelling as though the battle was to be fought with loud words.

"Attention — battalion!" said he, flourishing his sword. "Charge bayonets!"

"Stop a minute, Tommy!" called Major Toppleton, senior.

"Forward — march!" added Major Tommy, regardless of his father's interference.

"Hold on a minute, Tommy!" repeated his father. "I want to see you."

"Forward — march!" screamed the little major, desperately. "Now give them fits! Don't mind a scratch! Drive them before you!"

"Charge bayonets!" cried Major Waddie, on the other side; and it was clear enough that he did not intend to run away.

In vain did Major Toppleton senior attempt to check this forward movement. The Toppletonians dashed gallantly up the hill, rushing upon the enemy with an impetuosity which threatened them with total annihilation. But then the Wimpletonians began to move forward; and I felt my heart rising up into my throat, and my blood growing cold in my veins, as the combatants approached each other. I could almost hear the groans of the wounded, and see the outstretched forms upon the green sod, so real did the scene appear to me.

The two lines met, and I heard the clatter of cold steel as the bayonets struck against each other; but I had not time to form an exact idea of what was going on before I saw the Toppletonians give way in the centre. It was a confused *mêlée*, and I could only see a general punching and hammering with the muskets. When I saw a soldier on either side make a direct thrust with his bayonet, it was warded off with a blow. Indeed, the battle seemed to be fought literally "at the point of the bayonet;" for, so far as I could judge, neither party went near enough to do any damage. Each side seemed to have the requisite discretion to keep out of the reach of the weapons of the other side. I think there were not many in either rank that had the ferocity actually to wound their adversaries with the weapons in their hands.

This was the beginning of the affray, and the contending forces had not yet become desperate; and, though they rushed upon each other with appalling savageness, as seen by the observer, the contest was at a safe distance, neither party permitting the other to come near enough actually to inflict wounds. In fact, it was just such fighting as I had often seen between parties of boys, and consisted in rushing up and falling back. Dangerous as the weapons were, there was really no blood-thirsty spirit on either side.

The Toppletonian centre was broken. Captain Bayard had been pressing things, and the force in front of him, to avoid any actual punching of the bayonets, fell back. Major Waddie strode furiously up and down his line — in the rear of it, of course — yelled, and stormed, and gesticulated. When he saw the centre in front of him give way, he screamed in his fury, and Bayard, who seemed to have some of the spirit of his illustrious namesake, forced his

company forward till some of them were actually pricked by the steel of the Toppletonians. But this spurring seemed only to infuriate them ; Waddie yelled louder than ever, and Bayard, perceiving his advantage, encouraged his soldiers till the line before them yielded, and were swept backward down the hill.

Captain Pinkerton, on the right, inspired by the success of the centre, and goaded on by the frantic yells and gestures of Major Waddie, crowded his company forward, and the line in front of him, whose equanimity was disturbed by the rupture of the centre, fell back also.

"Three cheers, and drive them !" roared Major Waddie, hoarsely, as his white plume flaunted in the fresh breeze.

Then the Wimpletonians yelled along the whole length of the line, and rushed down the hill, the demoralized Toppletonians fleeing before them. Major Toppleton and myself were obliged to retire in order to avoid the onslaught of the victorious battalion.

"The scoundrels !" ejaculated the great man, who

13

appeared to be quite as much disconcerted as his son.

"The Wimps have the best of it," I replied.

"This is disgraceful!" muttered the major.

I thought so myself; not the defeat, as he understood it, but the battle itself, as I understood it.

Near the camp of the Toppletonians was a belt of trees extending across the island, into which the discomfited battalion retreated. The Wimpletonians followed them closely, and I was afraid the camp and baggage of our boys would be captured by the enemy. In the shadow of the grove, Major Tommy and his two captains rallied the intimidated Toppletonians, and they made a stand under the friendly shelter of the trees, the enemy halting at the verge of the grove. The great man and myself hastened to headquarters, where we found Tommy breathless with rage and excitement at his unexpected defeat. His father taunted him upon his misfortune, which did not help his fiery mood.

"What could I do when the fellows gave way?" stormed he. "They are a pack of cowards, and would run a mile rather than be pricked with the point of a pin."

"It is easy enough for you to talk, Tommy Toppleton," snapped private Putnam. "If you went in the front instead of the rear, it would make a difference with you."

"I was in the place where a commander ought to be," retorted Tommy, stung by this reproach. "I will give you enough of it before you get through." ·

"You needn't call us cowards while you keep yourself in a safe place," added Putnam.

"Attention — battalion!" shouted Major Tommy, suddenly.

"What are you going to do now?" asked his father.

"I'm going to drive the Wimps into the lake this time."

"What's the use! If you go out of the grove, you will only be driven back," replied the major, senior.

"Why don't you make a flank movement?" I suggested.

"What do you mean by that?" asked Tommy, whose attention was arrested by the idea.

" Send one company round to the other side of the Wimps," I, replied.

" If I send half my men away, the Wimps will defeat the rest here."

" No; half your force can hold this wood. If you can get one company on the high ground, you will have the advantage over them."

Major Tommy thought favorably of the idea; and I thought it would be safer for both parties to fight the battle by running and manœuvring than for them to make a stand-up conflict on the open field, as they had done. Briscoe was sent with his company to make the flank movement. He double-quicked his command towards the east shore of the island, and began to ascend the slope. Major Waddie promptly " smelt a mice," and despatched Captain Bayard's company to watch and check the movements of the flanking force. I went with Briscoe, intent upon using whatever influence I had to keep the parties from coming into actual contact with each other. We reached the summit of the slope by hard running, in advance of Captain Bayard; and here the Toppleton company halted on the highest ground on the island.

"Now you are all right, Briscoe," said I. "Send half a dozen fellows to demonstrate against their boats, and you will get them out of the way."

"You do that, Wolf," replied he. "Go down, and shove them off, and I will do the rest."

I ran down the slope alone to the landing, where I found Colonel Wimpleton.

CHAPTER XVII.

THE PRISONER OF WAR.

COLONEL WIMPLETON was just landing from a boat, in which he had been ferried over from the main shore, having come from Centreport to this point in his chaise. As soon as he landed, he dismissed the man who had brought him over. The two great men of the vicinity were both on the island.

As soon as I left Captain Briscoe's company, and moved towards the landing-place, Bayard, in command of the Wimpleton company, evidently suspected my purpose, though I really had no intention of meddling with the boats, but only of making a demonstration. Half a dozen soldiers were sent in a hurry to guard the fleet. This was Briscoe's opportunity. The force before him was now reduced so that an attack was hopeful. I heard him shouting, and a moment later the company of Bayard came helter-skelter over the summit of the hill. Our fellows, mortified by their first defeat, had made a desperate charge, and driven the enemy before them. It was not safe, therefore, for me to meddle with the boats, even if I had intended to do so.

"How goes the battle, Wolf?" asked the colonel, with a smile, as I met him on the beach.

"Just now it seems to be going in favor of Toppleton," I replied; "though our boys were just driven half way across the island by yours."

"Well, that's good."

"But I can't stay here now, sir; I am afraid I shall be captured," I added, glancing at the six soldiers who were coming down the hill towards me.

"Don't be alarmed, Wolf; I will see that you are not hurt," laughed the colonel.

"I don't wish to be captured."

"You shall leave when you please. After thinking over the matter, I concluded that I should take our boys off the island," added the great man of Centreport; "but I don't intend to have them driven off."

"I'm very glad to hear it, sir."

"Where is Waddie?"

I explained the situation to him, and informed him of what had already transpired on the island. He was pleased with the victory which those who bore his name had achieved, and with this brilliant record of the Wimpleton battalion he was ready to retire. But while we were talking about the matter, the din of battle from the high ground saluted us. It appeared that Tommy Toppleton, too impatient to wait for the result of the flanking movement, had charged upon the company of Wimpletonians in front of him. Our fellows had wiped out the disgrace of the early part of the action, and had driven the enemy up the hill, over its summit, regaining all the ground lost, and taking the summit of the slope, which was "the key to the situation."

"This won't do," said Colonel Wimpleton, as he saw with dismay that his party was defeated. "I can't take them away under these circumstances."

But the battle was lost to the Wimpletonians. Major Tommy had gained the crown of the hill, and held it with his whole force. The ground was so steep in front of him that double the number of the foe could not dislodge him. The enemy had not yet pitched their tents, and their baggage was now in danger of capture. Major Waddie consolidated his battalion, and formed a line at the foot of the hill, ready to defend his camp equipage. He was furious at his defeat, and when he saw me his eyes flashed fire.

"Arrest that traitor!" said he, flourishing his sword, and pointing to me.

"Not yet, Waddie!" interposed his father. "I have given him a safe conduct."

"You are not in command here," replied the ungracious son. "What are you doing down here, Wolf Penniman?"

"I should have gone before if your father had not detained me."

"Keep cool, Waddie," said the colonel. "You have enough to do to whip the Toppletonians."

"That's what I'm going to do," added Major Waddie, as he glanced at the summit of the hill.

" I will take care of Wolf, and see that he don't whip the whole of you."

"I will hang him as a traitor if he don't start quick. He has no business over here."

" He is a non-combatant," laughed the colonel.

I do not know what the gallant commander of the Wimpleton battalion would have deemed it necessary to do with me, if the exigency of battle had not called his attention to other matters. I do not pretend to be a brave fellow, but I am willing to say I was not afraid of being hanged, even independently of the powerful protection of the colonel. Major Tommy, flushed with his recent success, was intent upon following up his victory. I heard him call his battalion to the charge, and the words induced my feathery persecutor to leave me. Tommy evidently intended to drive the enemy into the lake, or to force them to surrender on the shore.

" Charge — bayonets! Forward — march!" yelled he; and down came the Toppletonians at a furious pace.

" Now stand up to it, fellows!" screamed Waddie.

"This is your last chance. Don't run if they punch you through."

Not only Waddie, but the two captains in his battalion, who had more real influence than the commander, urged the Wimpletonians to stand firm, and not be driven from their position. But the time for argument was short. The victorious Toppletonians swept down the hill, and rushed furiously at the foe. This time I am quite sure there were some wounds given on both sides. Major Tommy, mortified, no doubt, by the taunts of Putnam, and perhaps of others, did not march in the rear of his column, but very imprudently placed himself in advance of it. Fortunately for him, there were several privates near him who were inspired by his gallant example, and the centre of the column broke through the enemy's front. This would have been a success to the Toppletonians if the right and left wings had supported the movement with equal zeal. They did not, and were forced back by the desperate Wimpletonians, and in a moment more were retreating up the hill, closely pursued by the enemy.

When it was too late, Tommy saw where he was.

He was standing, supported by only half a dozen privates, several rods in advance of his battalion. A squad of the enemy, led on by Captain Pinkerton, charged upon him. The daring little major defended himself with zeal and courage, slashing right and left with his sword. His supporters, seeing the situation, fell back and joined their companions. Closely pressed by his exultant foe, Tommy struck savage blows against the muskets of his asaulters; but suddenly his sword blade snapped off near the hilt.

"Capture him! Capture him!" shouted Pinkerton; and sending part of his squad behind Tommy, he cut off his retreat.

The gallant major was now unarmed, and incapable of making any defence. His companions in arms had been forced back to the summit of the hill.

"Surrender!" cried Pinkerton.

"Never!" yelled Tommy, with tragic grandeur, as he made a dive at the captain, with the intention apparently of wresting his sword from him.

Such bravery deserved a better fate; but two of the enemy came behind the impetuous major, and, grasping him by the shoulders, threw him down. The whole squad then fell upon him, and poor Tommy was a prisoner of war. Two of the stoutest of his captors, each of them half a head taller than he was, were detailed to guard the major, and he was marched to a tree near the camp baggage.

The Toppletonians were driven to the top of the hill, and resumed their position upon its summit. It was useless for the Wimpletonians to attempt to drive them beyond the ridge, and they returned to their former halting-place on the level ground. I began to be a little uneasy about the fate of Tommy when Major Feathers returned, for I was afraid the latter, inspired by no lofty ideas of military honor, would subject his prisoner to some indignities. I saw Waddie hold a conference with his two captains, the result of which was soon apparent. Captain Bayard, attended by a single private, who carried a white handkerchief suspended on a pole, as a flag of truce, walked up the hill. I was not informed until afterwards of the nature of their mission; but, in the opinion of the Wimpletonians, the capture of Tommy decided the fate of the day, and they regarded the battle as ended, with victory perched upon their banners. Major Waddie was graciously pleased to declare that he did not wish to pursue his conquest any farther, and if the Toppletonians would retire from the island, their commander should be returned to them unharmed.

By the misfortune of Major Tommy, Captain Briscoe was the ranking officer, and the message of Major Waddie was delivered to him. By the advice of Major Toppleton, senior, the terms of peace were promptly rejected, and an intimation given that the Toppletonians intended to recapture their commander, and drive the invaders into the deep waters of the lake. While these negotiations were in progress, Colonel Wimpleton left me, and went to the headquarters of the battalion. Doubtless he saw his powerful rival on the top of the hill, and wished to counteract the influence of his counsels with his own.

When the flag of truce returned, I saw a private run to the tree where Major Tommy had been secured with a rope taken from one of the boats. Then the two stout fellows in charge of him conducted him to a boat, and pushed off. It was intended that the commander of the Toppleton battalion should not be recaptured, and the threat of his forces was rendered futile. But his command immediately repeated the assault, when the nature of Colonel Wimpleton's advice was evident. The beach in the rear of the Centreport battalion was covered with small round stones, with which the soldiers had plentifully supplied themselves. The onslaught of the Toppletonians was received with a volley of these missiles. They reeled under this unexpected reception, and being on the grass they could not procure any similar ammunition. Captain Briscoe, imitating the example of his illustrious commander, marched in front. The stones seemed to be aimed at him, and he actually fell, hit by one of them. His forces, appalled at this savage warfare, and by the fall of their leader, halted, and then fell back beyond the reach of the mischievous missiles. Briscoe was picked up, and borne to the top of the hill. The affair was becoming more serious, and, I may consistently add, more disgraceful, especially as the contending parties were now virtually directed by Major Toppleton and Colonel Wimpleton, who were old enough to have known better.

It was plain enough that our boys could not stand up against these volleys of stones, and that the Wimpletonians could hold their ground for the rest of the week. The battle was now to be a matter of strategy and manœuvring. On the hill, as they saw Major Tommy sent off in the boat, they concluded that he was safe enough for the present, and were not disposed to accept any ignominious terms of peace. The two fellows in charge of the prisoner of war had pulled off a quarter of a mile from the shore, and were watching the issue of the combat. I was curious to know what would be done next, but I concluded to operate a little on my own account. Following the shore round the island, I reached the pier, and went on board of the yacht. Skotchley and Grace, in the standing-room, were watching the action, while Tom Walton and Joe Poole had gone up to the mast-head, where they could obtain a better view of the field of battle.

"All hands, unmoor!" I called, and my ready crew descended to the deck.

The mainsail had not been lowered, and we had only to get up the anchor and hoist the jib. Before the fresh breeze we stood down the channel towards the boat in which Tommy was an unwilling passenger.

14

CHAPTER XVIII.

RESCUING A PRISONER.

ON the passage I told Grace and Ned Skotch-ley what had transpired during the time I had been on shore; and both of them agreed with me that it was disgraceful to allow boys to fight. Grace even had the courage to say that her father ought to have compelled the Toppletonians to leave the island, rather than encourage such outrageous conduct.

"What are you going to do now?" asked Skotch-ley.

"I'm going to recapture Tommy."

"I thought you were a non-combatant," laughed he.

"So I am; but I'm not going to leave Tommy in the hands of those fellows. I'm afraid the Wimps will abuse him when they have time to attend to his case."

"Don't let them hurt him," pleaded Grace.

"I will not. Tommy is as brave as a lion; if he had been as prudent as Waddie, he would not have been captured," I replied.

By this time we were within hail of the boat in which the prisoner of war was held. His guards did not know the Grace, as she was a new craft on the lake, and did not expect any mischief from her. They sat on each side of the vanquished little major, whose hands were tied together so that he could do no harm. I ran the yacht up into the wind so that her bowsprit was over the boat.

"What are you about? You will run into us!" shouted one of the sentinels.

"We won't hurt you," replied Tom Walton, as he hooked on to the boat.

I ran forward, and Tom and I dropped into the boat, while Joe Poole held the painter, which I threw up to him to avoid accidents.

"Wolf Penniman!" exclaimed Baxter, one of the guards, when he recognized me. "What do you want?"

"I want Major Tommy," I replied, cutting that

young gentleman's fetters, while Tom Walton stood between me and the astonished sentinels.

"You can't have him! He is a prisoner," retorted Baxter, picking up his musket.

"He was a prisoner, but he isn't now," I added. "You are free, Tommy. Jump aboard as quick as you can."

But Raymond, the sentinel in the bow of the boat, presented his bayonet, while Tom Walton, with an oar in his hand, was checking a forward movement on the part of Baxter. It is not easy to walk over a bayonet in the hands of a stout fellow who has been trained to use it skilfully, and the prospect before me was not very encouraging. However, Joe Poole turned the fortunes of the day in our favor, by fastening to the back of Raymond's collar with the boat-hook, and pulling him over backwards into the bottom of the boat. I seized his musket, and wrenched it from his grasp, so that the obstacle to Major Tommy's escape was removed.

The little magnate was not slow to avail himself of his opportunity, and springing over the prostrate form of Raymond, still pinned down by the boat-hook, he leaped on board of the yacht. The combat, so far as I was concerned, was happily ended, and Tom Walton and I made good our retreat, which was effectually covered by Joe Poole, who flourished his boat-hook with a vigor that set at nought the paltry bayonets of the war-worn veterans from whose gripe we had rescued the unfortunate commander of the Toppleton forces.

"Don't let them go!" shouted Tommy, as he beheld the result of the brief struggle. "Capture them!"

"Let go the painter!" I whispered to Joe Poole.

"Capture them!" repeated Tommy, furiously, as he saw the boat recede from the yacht.

"Hard a-port the helm!" I called to Skotchley, who was in the standing-room.

"What are you about?" demanded Tommy, as I went aft to take the helm.

"Don't meddle with them, Mr. Wolf — don't, please!" interposed Grace.

"Shut up, Grace! If you say a word, I'll throw you overboard," said the ungallant major, who was unhappily one of those boys who believe they may say anything to a sister.

"I came out here after you, Tommy," I replied, indignant at the harsh words the little major had addressed to Grace. "I don't think it is worth while to meddle with those fellows."

"What do you suppose I care what you think!" cried Tommy. "Isn't this my father's yacht?"

"It is your father's yacht."

"Then you will capture those fellows, or I will know the reason why," he added, stoutly.

"Don't touch them, Mr. Wolf — don't, please," said Grace.

"Mr. Wolf!" sneered Tommy. "Mr. Wolf will do what I tell him."

"I don't think it is quite proper to get into a row with a young lady on board!" I added, mildly.

"Wolf Penniman, you are a coward and a traitor!" exclaimed Tommy. "And you are another!" he added, fixing his indignant gaze upon Skotchley.

"Thank you, Tommy," replied the dignified student, coolly.

"You shall be court-martialed as a deserter and a coward!"

"Well, I think I can stand it."

Major Tommy glanced at the boat from which he had been removed, and in which his two guards had taken the oars and were pulling for the shore. He seemed to think that they would add two more to the force of the Wimpletonians, and that it was a grave military indiscretion to permit the enemy thus to be augmented. Besides, he must have his own way, and any opposition was quite enough to rouse the evil spirit in his nature. He insisted again that the two guards should be captured. I tried to excuse myself from meddling in the warfare, and Grace stood by me with a zeal which brought down the wrath of her brother upon her.

"I say that boat shall be taken," persisted he, violently.

"It is impossible," I replied, weary of his tyranny. "She is dead to windward of us."

"Please don't, Mr. Wolf," added Grace.

"Hold your tongue, Grace!" snapped he, as he sprang to the tiller, and shoved me one side,

"Don't, Tommy," added Grace, placing her hand upon his shoulder to deter him.

The little monster actually turned upon her, and struck her a blow in the face which sent her reeling over into her seat. I could not stand that; my blood boiled up, and boiled over. I sprang upon him, and in a small fraction of an instant, Major Tommy Toppleton was lying flat on the floor of the standing-room.

"O, don't touch him, Mr. Wolf!" begged Grace.

"You villain you, how dare you put your hand upon me?" gasped Tommy, springing to his feet, as savage as a young tiger.

"I don't like to see any one strike a young lady, least of all when she is his sister."

"I'll let you know!" whined he, crying with passion, as he leaped upon me.

Walton and Skotchley each grasped one of his arms, and held him so that he was powerless. He raved, tore, and swore; and it was evident enough to me, when my indignation subsided, that I had sacrificed myself, if not my father and the whole family,

"I won't say anything more, Tommy," interposed Grace, terrified by the violence around her. "You may have your own way."

"Give me that helm, Wolf!" cried Tommy.

"I will give it to you," I replied, moving aside, influenced by the action of Grace; and I don't know but Tommy would have beaten his head to jelly against the trunk if some concession had not been made to his wrath.

He cooled off as rapidly as he had become heated, when all opposition was removed. He threw the yacht up into the wind, and Tom Walton and I trimmed the sails; but the new helmsman could not manage her, and she lay with her sails flapping idly in the wind.

"Ease her off a little, Tommy, and she will go it," I ventured to suggest.

"Mind your own business, Wolf Penniman. Your time is out from this moment, and Grace shall never put her foot into this yacht again, if it is named after her," blustered Tommy.

I subsided, and seated myself on the trunk amidships to wait the issue. The new skipper, however, adopted my suggestion, though he snubbed me for making it. The Grace, accommodating as she was, would not sail into the wind's eye, and before Tommy was ready to tack, in beating up to the chase, the boat landed her hands on the beach. I saw that he was vexed; but he "chewed up" his wrath. He soon came about, and headed for the channel between the Horse Shoe and the Shooter. I concluded that he must be anxious to join his battalion; but it would be impossible to beat the yacht up the narrow passage. It was no use for me to say anything, and I did not, for he would be sure to go in direct opposition to any suggestion of mine.

He ran the Grace up to the north point of the Shooter, and came about. I thought it my duty to tell him that the water was very shoal ahead of him, as he approached the Horse Shoe on this tack. He politely insinuated that I was to hold my tongue, which I succeeded in doing for a moment longer, until the yacht grated on the gravel bottom, and stuck fast.

"That's just where I wanted her," said Tommy, unmoved by the event. "Joe Poole!"

Joe Poole appeared before the imperious little magnate, and was directed to bring up the boat and land our uncomfortable passenger. Tommy jumped into the boat, and as he took his seat in the stern-sheets, he delivered his parting volley at me, to the effect that, like Othello, my occupation was gone, and that I should be driven out of Middleport as a coward and a traitor. To this mild speech I permitted myself to make no reply.

"Hurrah! Hurrah! Hurrah!" shouted the Toppleton battalion on the shore.

This shout of triumph attracted the attention of the major, and he hurried up Joe Poole, who soon landed him on the beach. On the whole, I concluded that I had not made much by meddling with the conflict, even so far as to rescue Tommy from his captors. During the events which I have related, I had closely watched the movements of the contending forces. Company B of the Toppleton battalion had been sent round the island to flank the enemy, and obtain a position where stones were available as ammunition. This operation had been successful, and the Wimpletonians had been

forced back from their stronghold, for they could
not stand up against volleys of stones any better
than their rivals. Company A had dashed down
the hill at the right time, and the enemy were
driven upon their baggage. This success had drawn
forth the shout of triumph.

Fortunately for us on board of the Grace, Tommy had sailed her shaking in the wind, so that she
had gone on the shoal very gently, though hard
enough to give us two hours of severe exertion.
As we worked, moving ballast from the forward to
the after part of the yacht, we watched the movements of the contending forces. As I anticipated,
Tommy ordered another charge as soon as he
reached the battalion, though the Wimpletonians
were actually engaged in loading their baggage
into the boats. We saw a flag of truce hoisted by
the defeated party, and a parley took place, the
result of which was, that they were permitted to
retire without further molestation. Long and loud
were the cheers of Toppleton when the fleet moved
away from the island, and pulled towards the
Shooter. The victors then returned to their camp.

We got the Grace off at last, and, after passing around the Horse Shoe, I anchored off the pier in the channel. Major Toppleton soon appeared, accompanied by Tommy, and I expected to be discharged at once.

CHAPTER XIX.

A TYRANNICAL SON.

"I SUPPOSE my time is out, Miss Toppleton," said I to Grace, as I saw the big major and the little major approaching the pier.

"Your time out?" she replied, looking anxiously at me.

"I shall be discharged from my situation, and perhaps be driven out of Middleport."

"O, no! I hope not, Mr. Wolf."

"Tommy is very arbitrary, and after what has happened, he will not permit me to remain on the same side of the lake with him."

"I am sorry you touched him," said she, musing.

"I should not have touched him if he had struck me. I was indignant and angry."

"Well, I don't blame you, Mr. Wolf, for it is abominable for a boy to strike his sister," she added, placing her hand upon her pretty face, where her brother's rude hand had left its mark. "But Tommy rules the whole house at home; and I suppose he will have his own way now, as he always did."

As Tommy got into the boat which I had sent for him and his father, I saw that he was still in a very unamiable frame of mind. He was talking loudly and indignantly to his father, who appeared to be trying to soothe him and moderate his wrath. For my own part, I could not regret what I had done, unpleasant as the consequences promised to be. It was not in my nature to stand by and see a little bully, like Tommy, strike a young lady, — not pat her gently, but strike her a heavy blow, — not even if he were her brother. I had been tempted to give the young ruffian the pounding which he richly deserved, and to continue the operation until he was willing to promise better things.

Perhaps the handsome offer which Colonel Wimpleton had made me rendered me somewhat more independent than I should otherwise have been. I was certainly in good condition to be discharged, and did not feel much like submitting to any gross indignities from the great man of Middleport, or his hopeful son. But Major Toppleton had been very kind to me, and to my father, and I could not forget the service he had rendered to us.

The boat came alongside, and Tommy leaped upon the deck, followed by his father; and I could not help noticing that the senior major looked very anxious and uncomfortable. Tommy had doubtless been making strong speeches to him, and it was really melancholy to think of a man of his abilities, dignity, and influence reduced to a kind of slavery by the tyranny of his own son; and all the more melancholy because he could not realize that he was spoiling the boy by this weak indulgence.

" Wolf Penniman," said the little major, majestically, " I always keep my promises."

" Keep cool, Tommy," interposed his father, stepping into the standing-room, where Grace and I were seated alone, for Skotchley and Tom Walton had gone forward.

" You know what I said, father. I won't have Wolf around me any longer. He has been a coward and a traitor, and he had the audacity to knock me down. Wolf Penniman, you are discharged!" continued Tommy, blustering furiously.

"Don't be too fast, Tommy," interposed his father. "Wolf went after the boat in which you were a prisoner, captured it, and restored you to your command. Captain Briscoe told you that he did not dare to make his last move till he saw that Wolf had taken you out of the hands of the enemy."

"I don't blame him for that; but he refused to obey my orders, and then knocked me down. I say you may discharge him, or discharge me."

The alternative was a reminder of the Hitaca incident, and a hint that, if his father did not obey orders, Tommy would run away again, and there would be no suitable person to inherit the great man's millions. I made no reply, but bowed meekly to my fate. It appeared that, after all, I was not to run the Lightning Express train, about which so much had been said.

"Don't let him discharge Mr. Wolf, father," interposed Grace, her pretty cheeks red with indignation; and with such an advocate I could afford to be still.

15

" Discharge Mr. Wolf!" sneered the little magnate. "Will you learn to mind your own business,
Grace?"

"He struck me in the face, father, and that was
the reason why Mr. Wolf knocked him down. I am
sorry he did so, but I think Tommy was to blame,"
continued Grace.

"You needn't stick up for him; if you do, it
won't make any difference."

"I am astonished that you should strike your
sister," added Major Toppleton, whose painful expression fully proved his sincerity.

"Well, you needn't be!" replied Tommy, rudely
and disrespectfully. "If she don't mind her own
business, and let my affairs alone, I shall teach her
better. I have said all I have to say, and I'm
going ashore to look out for my battalion. Remember, Wolf is discharged!"

Tommy abruptly left the yacht, and, leaping into
the boat, ordered Joe Poole to pull him ashore.
The fiat had gone forth. I was discharged. Tommy was the president of the road, and doubtless he
had the power to dismiss me.

" Here is trouble," said Major Toppleton, with a sigh.

"I hope you won't let Mr. Wolf be discharged," said Grace, when the irate little magnate was out of hearing.

" What can I do ? " replied the major, impatiently. " Tommy is the president of the road, and he has the right to discharge an employee. If I interfere, there will be such a tempest as we had a year ago."

Poor magnate ! How I pitied him ! Just as I had seen a baby tyrannize over its loving mother, so did Tommy tyrannize over his father. The great man — how little he seemed to be then ! — mused for a while over the unpleasant situation.

" I'll tell you what we can do, Wolf. I want a skipper for this boat. If you will withdraw from the railroad for a time, I will give you this situation, with the same pay you are now receiving."

"I am entirely satisfied, sir, and shall be, whatever you or Tommy may do," I answered, meekly. "I certainly like the boat better than the train; but I suppose Tommy will not permit me to take charge of her."

The major bit his lips with vexation. His fetters

galled him, and he had not the resolution to shake
them off. He ordered me to get the yacht under
way, and start for Middleport. As soon as she was
clear of the narrow channel, the major asked me
down into the cabin, and we had a talk, which
lasted till the Grace came to anchor before the
owner's mansion.

"You know how I'm situated, Wolf," said he,
turning his gaze from me, as if ashamed to acknowledge his subservience to the wilful boy. "Tommy
must have his own way; he is desperate if he does
not. He will run away, or drown himself in the
lake, if he does not."

I could not help smiling at the infirmity of the
father, and he made haste to defend himself. Tommy was subject to fits when he was a child, and he
was fearful that irritation would bring on a return
of the malady. The young gentleman had actually
threatened to commit suicide if he could not have
his own way.

"I only wish to smooth the thing over for a time,
for Tommy is a good-hearted boy, and he will come
to his senses if he is not thwarted," added he.

"You are not a father, Wolf, and you can't understand the matter."

"I am willing to do whatever you desire, sir," I replied. "Perhaps I ought to say, that I can afford to be discharged just now. You have used me very handsomely, Major Toppleton, and I am grateful for your kindness. I will never leave your service of my own accord. Last night Colonel Wimpleton told me about his new steamer, which is to run in opposition to our Lightning Express, and offered me a man's wages to go either as engineer or as captain of her. I told him I could not leave my friends while they used me so well, and declined the offer. I did not mean to tell you of this, and should not, if things had not turned out just as they have."

The major bit his lip again. He was disposed to be angry; and, in a passion, he was as nearly like Tommy as one pea is like another. But he did not give way to the inclination.

"I declined the offer," I repeated, when I saw him struggling with the mischief within him.

"When will that steamer be ready to run?" he asked.

"In a couple of months, the builder told me."

"I'm glad you told me of this," he continued, after chewing upon it for some time. "Perhaps it will have some influence upon Tommy."

And there the matter ended for the present. Grace said she would do all she could for me; and however the rest of the house might regard me, I felt sure of an earnest advocate in her. She went on shore with her father, and as the skipper of the yacht, I spent the rest of the day in working upon her, and in putting down a set of moorings for her.

The next day I took a party up the lake in her, and for the rest of the week I was kept busy in my new occupation. I acquitted myself to the satisfaction of my employers, not only in pleasant weather, but in a heavy squall, which caught us in the middle of the widest part of the lake, off Gulfport.

The Wimpletonians encamped on the Shooter after they were driven from the Horse Shoe. The combat of Monday was not decisive enough to satisfy them, and the war was renewed, and continued during the week, with varying success. Each party stole the boats of the other, and inflicted whatever mischief it could. On Thursday night, in the midst of a violent storm, when the .Toppleton Guards sought shelter in their tents, the invading hordes of Wimpletonians crossed the channel, and actually conquered the territory of their rivals. Having levelled their tents, cut the cords, and broken up the tent-poles, they retired, satisfied with the mischief they had done. The Toppletonians were defeated in a similar attempt to invade the Shooter the next night; and when the end of the week arrived, neither could claim any material advantage over the other. The Wimpletonians had retrieved the disaster of the first day, and would have held the island if they had not been afraid of the interference of the owner.

Both parties returned to their studies, their hatred of each other not a jot abated, and more than ever before the Toppletonians were on the lookout for some opportunity to spite the other side.

When the battalion returned on Saturday night, I was up the lake in the Grace, and I did not see Major Tommy for several days. When we did meet,

he seemed to have forgotten everything that had
happened; but Grace told me she had listened to
the conversation between her father and him relating to the affair with me. At first the young
gentleman was furious at the idea of retaining me
in the yacht; but when he heard of Colonel Wimpleton's offer he yielded the point, and permitted
me to remain.

On the 1st of September the Lake Shore Railroad
was completed. Lewis Holgate had run the dummy
while I was skipper of the yacht; but the major
would not permit him to go on the locomotive, and
I was summoned back to my old position without
opposition from the little magnate.

CHAPTER XX.

THE LIGHTNING EXPRESS TRAIN.

THERE was something about Tommy's actions which I did not like. Though he spoke to me, as before, the old grudge was not wiped out. I saw that he and Lewis Holgate were very thick together, and I soon found that my fireman had ceased to be as tractable as at first. I heard he had reported among the boys that I was a Wimpletonian at heart, and would sell out the Lake Shore Railroad to the other side any time when I could get a chance.

The road was completed, and I ran the first train through to Ucayga. Major Toppleton had altered the Middleport into a ferry-boat at my suggestion, and she plied, in connection with the railroad, from our station on one side of the river to the town on the other. When we had gone over the ground a few times, the major sprang the trap. The two

boats which ran the whole length of the lake were
advertised to start from Middleport, touching at Centreport. Passengers from the latter place could cross
in one of them, and go by the railroad to Ucayga
— they could, but they did not like to do so. The
steamers plied in connection with the road, and the
Centreporters were as angry as though they had
been shut out from the rest of the world; for their
splendid boat was not yet ready to run in opposition to the new arrangement.

On Monday morning the Lightning Express train
was to make its first trip. Major Toppleton told me
to be sure and "make time." The track had been
carefully examined, and strengthened where it was
weak. I was to prove to the Centreporters that a
steamboat could not compete with the Lake Shore
Railroad. Everybody was excited, and the president
of the road absented himself from school, in order
to see that the programme was properly carried out.
I could have dispensed with his services; but he
insisted upon riding on the foot-board, probably to
see that I did not sell out the concern to the other
side.

"The cars are full, Wolf," said Tommy, after I had backed the locomotive into the station, and the cars were shackled to it.

"I am glad to hear it," I replied.

"I saw quite a number of people from the other side among the passengers."

"So much the better. We shall convince them that we can make time on this side of the lake."

Turning suddenly as I made this remark, I saw Lewis Holgate give Tommy a significant wink. I did not understand what it meant, and it troubled me a little. I should have been very glad to get rid of my fireman; but he was on such intimate terms with the president that it was useless for me to say anything. He did not attend to his duty, did not keep the working parts of the engine well oiled, and even neglected his fires. In fact, he had risen above his business since he had run the dummy.

"All aboard!" shouted the gentlemanly conductor, as he gave me the signal to start.

As I always did before I let on the steam, I glanced at the machinery around me. The reversing lever had been changed since I adjusted it. It must have been done by one of my companions in the cab. I restored the lever to its proper position for going ahead, and opened the throttle valve. The train started, but it went heavy. The engine acted weak. Glancing at the steam gauge, I saw that it indicated only three quarters of the necessary pressure.

"How's your fire?" I asked of Lewis.

"Good!"

"Look at it and see. The steam is low."

He obeyed me; but I saw that he put hardly a spoonful of coal into the furnace, and closed the door, while I was looking out ahead. The train went well down the grade; but when we approached Spangleport, we dragged hard.

"Fill up your furnace, Lewis," said I, rather sharply, as I observed that the gauge had hardly gained anything.

He put another spoonful of coal into the furnace.

"Fill it up!" I added, warmly; and I began to feel that some one was trying to sell me out.

"It won't burn if I put in too much," growled Lewis.

"Shovel it in," I continued, glancing into the fire box, which was nearly empty.

"More yet," I added, as he attempted to close the door.

I kept my eye on him till I was satisfied that we should soon have all the steam we could use. When I stopped the train at Spangleport we had lost five minutes, and, what was worse, I had nearly lost my temper. Lewis Holgate appeared to be laboring for the defeat, rather than the success, of the Lightning Express train. The presence of Mr. President Tommy on the foot-board seemed to be a partial explanation of his conduct. But I was determined that the enterprise should not be a failure. I was fully resolved to make time if steam could do it. Lightning Express was on trial, and if it failed, the Centreporters, whom I was now accused of favoring, would take courage.

We stopped but a moment at Spangleport. I opened the furnace, and stirred up the fire myself. At the same time I kept one eye on Lewis, and the other on Tommy; for I wanted to catch one of them reversing a crank, or doing any other mischief. Both of them looked innocent, though I saw them exchanging significant glances. By this time I had

a full head of steam, and was satisfied that I could
make up the lost time, if no further obstacles were
thrown in my way. The eight miles of road between Spangleport and Grass Springs was almost as
straight as an arrow, and I expected to recover the
lost ground on this run. Only an hour had been
allowed for the passengers to reach Ucayga. If the
train was behind time, those going east and west
would lose their passage.

"All aboard!" shouted the conductor, as he gave
me the signal to start the train.

"You are on time, Wolf, and you needn't hurry
yourself," said Tommy, as he consulted his watch.

"There's time enough," I replied, determined not
to be deceived by him.

I was nervous and excited, for I was conscious
that both of my companions on the engine were
laboring to make the Lightning Express a failure
in my charge. I kept my hand on the lever of the
throttle valve, almost afraid that it would be wrenched
from my grasp. I let on the steam, and kept letting
it on till the Ucayga — for that was the name which
had been given to the locomotive, in compliment to

the place which it was necessary to conciliate —
seemed to fly through the air.

"Shovel in the coal, Lewis," said I to my unwilling fireman, while we were rushing on at this furious
rate.

"I think there is enough coal in the furnace," replied he, opening the door.

"I don't think so. Shovel it in!"

He put in about half a shovel full, and did it
so doggedly that I was fully convinced he was
laboring to defeat the experiment. I spoke to him
very sharply. I threatened to stop the train, and
send for Major Toppleton.

"I am the president of this road. If you have
any complaints to make, you will make them to
me," interposed Tommy, who was holding on to the
cab with both hands.

"Will you tell the fireman, then, to do his duty?"

"He is doing it."

"Will you tell him to put in more coal?"

"Fill it up, Lewis," added Tommy, who seemed
to be conscious that there was a point beyond which
even he could not go.

My rascally assistant then attempted to choke the fires by overloading the furnace; but I watched him, and succeeded in preventing him from doing the mischief he intended.   I continued to increase the speed of the Ucayga until, I think, we were going at the rate of forty miles an hour. Tommy's hair stood on end, and so did my own, for that matter; but I was desperate.   I blew a long whistle as we approached Grass Springs.   When I shut off the steam I looked at my watch. We had made the eight miles in twelve minutes, and the train was on time when we went into the Springs.   I was satisfied then.

The moment the engine stopped, Tommy jumped off. He did not say anything, but I was convinced that he did not like riding on the locomotive, going at lightning-express rates. I was glad to get rid of him. I need not say that the events of the morning made me very uncomfortable. I had seen but little of Tommy since the events on the Horse Shoe; but I was conscious that he was nursing his wrath against me. Long before this time he would have driven me out of Middleport if he had not been so unpopular himself among the boys. My friend Dick Skotchley — for as such I was proud to regard him — had fought my battle for me among the students. Tommy was so conceited and overbearing that all the fellows hated him; and they were ripe for a mutiny against him in his capacity as president of the road, as well as in that of major of the battalion. More than this, Tommy's father was still my friend, though he feared his son. Without egotism I may say that I was popular in Middleport. If I had not been, I should have been kicked out, like a dog, by my imperious little master.

"How are you, Wolf?" shouted Tom Walton, as I was about to start the train.

"Jump on, Tom," I replied, as the conductor gave the word to go ahead.

My friend leaped into the cab, and I let on the steam. He told me he was spending a few days with his aunt at the Springs, and that he was looking for something to do. He was an active, industrious, quick-witted fellow, who never needed to be told twice how to do the same thing. Though he knew nothing about an engine, he had the abili-

16

ty to learn, and it immediately occurred to me that he would make a first-rate fireman, for it was evident that Lewis Holgate and myself could not much longer stand together on the same foot-board.

"This is bully — isn't it, Wolf?" said Tom, as the engine attained her highest speed, though, as there were now occasional curves, I was obliged to ease her a little at times.

"Do you like it?" I inquired.

"First rate. It is almost as good as the Grace — not quite," replied he, with proper enthusiasm. "Is this the Lightning Express folks talk so much about?"

"This is the Lightning Express. We have come through in a hurry this time. Five minutes' delay would ruin the Lake Shore Railroad, and cause more crowing over at Centreport than ten thousand roosters could do in a year. But we are on time."

"I'm glad you are," laughed Tom. "I expect the train will always be on time while you run it."

"If nothing happens, I shall put my passengers down in Ucayga at the time promised."

"I hope nothing will happen, then."

But at that very instant, before he had finished the remark, I saw, as we shot round a curve, a little child at play between the two rails. A woman was running towards it in frantic haste. My blood froze with horror. At first I felt like fainting; but I closed the valve and whistled to put on the brakes.

"Jam down that brake, Lewis!" I gasped to the fireman, indicating the one on the tender.

Tom Walton did not say anything, but passing through the window in the cab, he made his way to the cow-catcher. I grasped the reversing levers, and I think all the passengers must have been thrown off their seats when I checked the train. But it was still doubtful whether I could stop in season to save the child, and my heart was in my mouth.

CHAPTER XXI.

MAKING UP TIME.

IT seemed to me, if the locomotive ran over that child, that I could not have the audacity to live another day, though it would not be my fault. It was so awful, so horrible, that I prayed to be saved from the catastrophe. I did not feel as though I could ever hold up my head again if that innocent little child was sacrificed. It would be better that the Lake Shore Railroad should be sunk at the bottom of the lake than that a single precious life should be lost.

My blood ran cold through my veins as I gazed at the little child, who seemed to be paralyzed with astonishment as the iron monster swept towards her. It was a little girl, not more than four or five years old. The woman who ran shrieking towards the track was doubtless her mother. What a moment of agony it was to her! My heart bled for her, and the triumph of the Lightning Express sank into insignificance as I contemplated the thrilling scene.

As the engine came nearer to the little girl, my hopes rose higher, for our speed was effectually checked by the efforts we had made. Tom Walton was on the cow-catcher, and I knew that he would do the right thing at the right time. The child showed no disposition to move; indeed, I think she had no power to do so, even if she comprehended the nature of her peril. As we came near enough, I saw her eyes set in a kind of fixed stare, which indicated astonishment rather than fear.

"Jam down the brakes, Lewis!" I called to the fireman, as I labored to check the speed of the engine; and I must do him the justice to say that he was not at all backward in obeying my order, though I doubt whether he would have been equally zealous if it had been I, instead of the child, who was on the track.

The speed of the train was checked, but it was not stopped; and so far as the life of the child was concerned, we might as well have been going at the rate of forty as five miles an hour, for the slightest blow of the cow-catcher would have killed her. All this transpired within a few seconds. Hardly an instant elapsed after the steam was shut off, and the brakes put on, before I was trying to back the engine. The sparks flew under the drive-wheels, but still the iron mass swept on towards the child, whose instants appeared to be numbered. It seemed to me that I stopped breathing as the little child disappeared behind the forward part of the locomotive. I expected to hear a shriek — to be conscious that the child was a gory, mangled, and shapeless mass beneath.

Almost at the same moment, Tom Walton straightened up, holding the child in one arm. The engine had almost stopped, and was still groaning and struggling under my ineffectual labors to bring it to a complete stand. My heart leaped the instant I saw the child in the arms of my friend. My blood, rolled back by the fearful suspense, seemed to be bursting through my veins, and I was disposed to shout for joy.

"She is safe!" cried Tom, at the top of his voice, as he leaped from the engine upon the ground, and placed the little girl in the arms of her mother.

I saw the horror-stricken parent press the little one to her bosom. I heard the sob of convulsive agony which attended the tremendous reaction. It was like passing from death to life for her, and I felt that I could almost understand even a mother's emotion.

"Thank God! Thank God!" I cried; and they were not idle words that I uttered, for it seemed to me that the Good Father had interposed to save me from what I should have remembered with horror all the rest of my life.

I could not but regard it as an interposition of Providence in my favor, rather than the child's; but in the mother's favor rather than that of either of us, for she would have been the greatest sufferer. I am sure this incident had a powerful influence upon me, not for the moment, or the day only, but for all the rest of my life. It has kept my eyes open when I was disposed to close them; it has decided the question of running a risk when nothing else seemed to restrain me; it taught me to regard human life as too sacred to be trifled with.

I saw the fond mother clasp her child, and with the reaction came the thought that I was running the Lightning Express train; that the reputation of Middleport depended upon the time I should make.

"Jump on, Tom!" I called to my friend, as he paused for a moment to gaze at the mother and her rescued child.

"That was a narrow squeak!" said he; and the whole face of the generous fellow expanded into one smile of satisfaction.

"It was, indeed, Tom," I replied, as I let on the steam, and whistled to take off the brakes. "It was a merciful providence that you were on the engine with me. If you had not been, the child would have been dead at this instant."

"I am glad I was here, then. I think that woman will keep her child in the house after this," replied he.

I crowded on the steam again, and once more the train flew like the wind along the lake shore. All the time I was thinking of that little child; of the anguish that would have filled that cottage by the lake, at this moment, if Tom Walton had not happened to be on the engine with me. I could have done no more than I did do, and though the train was on the very point of stopping, there was still momentum enough left in it to have crushed the little one to death. I was grateful to God as I had never been before for sparing me such a calamity.

In the exhilaration of the moment I urged forward the locomotive till I saw the steamer which was waiting to convey the passengers across the river. I looked at my gold watch, thought of Grace Toppleton, as I always did when I glanced at its face, and almost forgot why I had taken it from my pocket in thinking of the expression of her beautiful face when I should relate to her the thrilling incident which had just occurred. I was on time; I was ahead of time, for I had driven the engine at a furious speed. But I had worked carefully;

I had favored it on the curves, and I felt as safe myself as if I had been in my father's house.

The brakes were put on, and the train stopped at the rude pier which had been built for the steamer. Major Toppleton had carefully instructed Captain Underwood, and the boat was ready to start on the instant. Hardly had the cars stopped before the deck hands began to load the baggage on the trucks. Everybody worked as if the salvation of the nation depended upon his individual exertions, and I am afraid that some of the passengers had occasion to weep as they saw the rude manner in which their baggage was tossed about. I do not think it would have taken a moment longer for the men to handle the trunks respectfully — for this seems to me to be the proper word, since the feelings of the traveller are so largely centred in his luggage.

Major Toppleton stood on the platform, and drove up the men. He did not seem to care whose trunk was smashed if he only succeeded in carrying out his own plans. He had allowed just one hour for the transportation of the passengers from Middleport to the station in Ucayga, and I think he would cheerfully have given ten thousand dollars rather than fail in the enterprise.

Tommy stood on the platform near his father; but there was no expression of satisfaction on his face. He had labored to defeat the enterprise in order to overwhelm me. It was disaster to him, and I am inclined to think he was still holding in lively remembrance the disobedience of which I had been guilty three months before.

The trucks, piled high with trunks and valises, were wheeled on the forward deck of the Middleport, from which they could be rolled to the baggage car on the other side when the train arrived. The boat started. The long experience of Captain Underwood enabled him to clear or make a landing in the shortest possible time. But fifteen minutes had been allowed for getting the passengers over, and I had the satisfaction of seeing the trucks on the platform upon the other side of the river full five minutes before the train was due. My anxiety had come to an end. I looked upon the Lightning Express as a glorious triumph, and, in contrast with it, I could not help thinking how cheap and mean we should have felt if the train had rushed off before the passengers arrived. The failure would have been charged upon me, and I am afraid I could not have saved myself by exposing the conspiracy which had been instigated by Tommy.

The trains from the east and from the west, which passed each other at Ucayga, were both on time, as they generally were. I saw the truck unloaded, then loaded again with the baggage of the passengers who were going up the lake, and in a few moments the Middleport was crossing the river. The train was to leave at quarter past ten, but the promptness of the steamer's people allowed me five minutes of grace. Lewis had left the engine, when he knew that it was his duty to "oil up," and I was performing this work myself, when Major Toppleton came up, his face beaming with smiles. My fireman was talking with Tommy on the platform.

"Well, Wolf, this works to a charm," said the magnate, rubbing his hands with satisfaction.

"Yes, sir; we came through on time, after all,"

I replied, as I poured the oil on one of the piston rods.

"I heard there was a child on the track this side of the Springs."

"Yes, sir; Tom Walton, who was on the engine with me, went out on the cow-catcher and saved it. I think we should have lost the trip if Tom had not been with me," I continued, fully explaining the exciting incident.

"Tom is a good fellow, and he always has his head near the ends of his fingers," answered the major.

I wanted to tell him that Tommy and my fireman had done what they could to defeat the great enterprise; but I concluded that it would be useless to do so, for the son was the master. I had made a good impression in Tom Walton's favor, and I reserved my next step till a more convenient season.

CHAPTER XXII.

THE NEW FIREMAN.

"ALL aboard!" shouted our bustling conductor, who was a very gentlemanly young man, and had had considerable experience in this capacity.

He wore a gold badge on the lapel of his coat, wrought in the shape of a train of cars, on which was inscribed the word "Conductor," in such curious old English text that no one who did not know what it was could read it. He alleged that the jewel had been presented to him by a host of admiring passengers; but those who knew him best declared that he had spent a whole month's salary in 'its purchase. It was a very pretty thing, and, wherever he got it, he was certainly polite enough to have merited it.

The gentleman with the gold jewel bowed, and

gracefully made the signal to me; and, after glancing at the reversing handle, I grasped the throttle valve, ready to start. At this moment Lewis sprang upon the footboard. I had attended to the fire myself, and was thoroughly disgusted with the conduct of my fireman.

"Stop!" shouted Tommy, imperiously.

It was the president of the road who spoke, and I was obliged to obey.

"It is against the rules of the road for any one to ride on the engine," continued the little magnate.

"I never heard of any such rule before, Mr. President, or I should not have disregarded it," I replied, as gently as I could, though I know my face flushed with indignation.

"I make the rule now, then," added Tommy.

"Tom is only going to Grass Springs with me," I ventured to suggest.

"He shall not ride on the engine. Conductor, you will collect his fare," replied Tommy, glancing at the gentlemanly person with the gold jewel.

"Wolf, I haven't a red cent in my trousers pocket; but I suppose I can walk to the Springs," said my friend, who knew how vain it would be to appeal against the orders of the magnificent little president.

I slipped half a dollar into his hand, and he jumped down.

"Have you the money to pay your fare?" demanded the gentlemanly conductor, for he was ready enough to "spoony" to the president.

"I have," answered Tom, with dignity, as he stepped into the forward car.

It was a gratuitous insult to me, and Lewis Holgate chuckled with delight. I bit my lips with vexation; but I said nothing — it was of no use to say anything. Even Major Toppleton himself would not have dared to dispute the fiat of his son.

"All right!" cried the conductor; and I started the train, a minute behind time.

I was vexed and unhappy. I felt like a free man reduced to slavery. I had lost Tommy's favor, and I was nobody, though everybody else praised me. I felt that I had done my duty to the road, and to Middleport in general. I had worked hard at electioneering to keep Tommy in his position as president. I had supported him to the best of my ability; but he insulted me without remorse. I could not help thinking that it was stupid and servile in me to stand it; and I did not think I could endure another snubbing without resenting it. I felt weak and ashamed of myself, especially as Colonel Wimpleton was still anxious to have me go in the new steamer.

I ran into Grass Springs on time, and Tom left the train, though not without saying a parting word to me. I wanted him to "fire" with me, and I had a plan in my mind to bring it about; but while the president of the road was bottling up his spite against me, I could hardly hope to gain my point.

The steamer for Hitaca was advertised to leave Middleport at eleven o'clock, and at the appointed hour I had the passengers on the wharf. Within a few moments of the time, the boat was off, and those who were bound to Centreport made the passage in an hour and a quarter from Ucayga, which was three quarters of an hour less than they had ever accomplished it before. Major Top-

17

pleton was more delighted than ever, and, though it was against the rules of the road for any one to ride on the engine, he jumped upon the footboard as lively as though he had been a boy. I ran up to the engine-house.

"It works splendidly, Wolf!" said the great man, rubbing his hands.

"It has come out right this time; but I think it is making rather close calculations," I replied, as we walked out of the building.

"What do you mean, Wolf?" he asked, anxiously, as though he feared there was still room for the great enterprise to fail, as indeed there was if Lewis Holgate continued on the engine with me.

"We have hardly five minutes to spare now, and the slightest accident might cause us to miss our connections."

"But with me the battle is to make the time to Ucayga inside of an hour. If it is more than an hour, it will sound bad, and we might just as well be an hour and a half as an hour and a quarter. I thought it was done handsomely this trip."

"Perhaps it was, sir; but I was five minutes

behind time when we reached Spangleport, and if I had not run at the rate of a mile in a minute and a half we should have missed the trains. Then the child on the track threw me back two minutes more, and compelled me to run the engine at its highest speed. The iron on the track is not heavy enough for such high rates."

"But why were you five minutes late at Spangleport?" asked the major.

Should I tell him why? It might endanger my place to bring a charge against Tommy; but I felt myself independent enough to do so.

"My fireman did not do his duty. I have been obliged to run the engine and fire too," I replied, explaining all that Lewis had done.

"What, Holgate! Discharge him then, at once," said the great man, impatiently.

"I am afraid that will not be so easy a matter," I added, with a smile.

"I think it will."

"Lewis does not act altogether on his own account, though he wants my place."

"Turn him off. Don't let him run another trip."

"I am sorry to say, sir, that Tommy is at the bottom of the mischief."

"Tommy?"

"Yes, sir."

I told him that Tommy had been working against me since the affair at the Horse Shoe; that he was trying to undermine me. The major was incredulous. Tommy was obstinate, he knew, but the president would not do anything to injure the Lake Shore Railroad. He was willing to believe that Lewis Holgate wished to get me out of my place, but not that his son was a party to the conspiracy.

"Lewis left the engine while we were waiting for the boat at Ucayga, and I should not have had steam enough to start the train if I had not shovelled in the coal myself. He did not even oil up, as he should have done, and as I told him to do," I continued.

"Discharge him, then."

"But all this time he was talking with Tommy; and you may be sure that your son will not permit him to be discharged."

Major Toppleton bit his lips. He was beginning

to comprehend the situation. He was actually afraid to carry his purpose into execution now, and, as I expected he would when the pinch came, he changed the subject of conversation, and said no more about getting rid of Lewis Holgate.

"I think, if we could save the two stops at Spangleport and Grass Springs, I could make the time without difficulty, even if we lost a few moments on the way," I suggested, as the entering wedge of the plan I had formed.

"But we can't neglect those two places. The people would tear up the rails if we failed to accommodate them."

"We will not neglect them. I suggest that you run the dummy half an hour before the Lightning Express for way passengers."

I explained fully my plan, and he was willing to adopt it, especially when I added that Lewis Holgate could handle the dummy very well indeed. He understood me then, and I thought I could see a smile of relief on his face.

"But you must have a fireman," he added.

"Yes, sir; and I would like to have Tom Walton. He is a faithful fellow, and learns quick."

"Engage him then at once. Who is the super-intendent now?"

"Wetherstane, sir."

He knew very well who the superintendent was, and knew also that he was one of the president's most bitter opponents. Wetherstane would discharge any one whom Tommy did like, or hire any one whom he did not like, without any scruples, and enjoy the operation. When the session of the Institute closed, the superintendent was waited upon by the major. I do not know what passed between them; but the next day posters in all the places on the line announced the new arrangement. Tom Walton was engaged.

In the afternoon I ran the Lightning Express through the second time. Tommy was not on the engine this time, and by closely watching my fire-man, I compelled him to do his duty; but without this care on my part, we should have failed in our connections. The next day, the last that Lewis was to run with me, for the new arrangement was to take effect on Wednesday morning, I found that the tender tanks were empty just as the engine

was to move down to the station for the train.
They had been filled an hour before, and I was
satisfied this was another trick to bring me into
disgrace. If I had not discovered the fact in season to correct the mischief, the trip would have
been lost, to say nothing of a worse calamity, if
anything could be worse in the estimation of the
major.

The pit under the track where the engine stood
was half filled with water, and it was evident enough
to me that my rascally fireman had uncoupled the
connecting hose while I was at dinner, and emptied
the tanks in this manner. I was provoked, and
disposed to pitch into the rascal. But this was
his last chance, I thought, and I concluded to
hold my peace. The scoundrel had probably drawn
off more of the water than he intended, or I might
not have discovered the condition of the tender in
season to fill it. But the train started on time, and
I was fortunate enough to make the connection at
Ucayga.

I had Tom Walton's appointment in my pocket,
and when we stopped at the Springs I gave it to

him, telling him to be at Middleport the next morning. This sharp movement had been prudently kept
from the president, and I hoped, as he would be in
school when the train started, that he would not ascertain what had been done until my friend had
made one or two trips.

The next morning, at half past eight, Lewis Holgate started the dummy for Ucayga. He was very
curious to know what I was going to do for a fireman; but I kept Tom in the shade till he was on
the way to the foot of the lake. There was to be
an awful row soon; but I was willing to postpone
it as long as possible. My friend was faithful and
intelligent, and before the train reached Ucayga, he
comprehended his duties. I made my time without
hurrying on this occasion.

In the afternoon, just as the Lightning Express
was to start on her second trip, Tommy rushed up
to the engine, looking as furious as a lunatic. At
Ucayga, where the dummy waited till the express
train had started, Lewis Holgate discovered who his
successor was. That Tom was a friend of mine was
enough to bring down upon him the wrath of the

president. With such an assistant, I was not likely to permit the Lightning Express to be a failure.

"What are you doing on that engine?" demanded Tommy.

"I fire on this engine now," replied Tom Walton, good-naturedly.

"No, you don't! not while I am president of the Lake Shore Railroad. Get off, and clear out!"

"If he leaves, I do," I interposed, quietly; but my blood was up.

Tommy looked at me, and ground his teeth with rage.

CHAPTER XXIII.

THE PRESIDENT AND THE ENGINEER.

IN five minutes it would be time for the Lightning Express train to start, and that was a very short time in which to fight the impending battle. Tommy was as unreasonable as a mule, and it was useless to attempt to conciliate him. Besides, I was tired of being buffeted by him. I was ashamed of my own servility, and much as I liked my occupation, I had deliberately come to the conclusion that it would be better for me to "hire out" for my board and clothes, than be a football for Tommy's capricious toes. I had always treated him respectfully and kindly; but he had insulted me a dozen times within a month.

"Are you the president of the Lake Shore Railroad?" demanded Tommy, violently.

"I haven't that honor," I replied.

"Then it is not for you to say who shall and who shall not run on the engine."

"That is very true; but it *is* for me to say whether I will run on it myself or not. Tom Walton was regularly appointed by the superintendent to fire on this engine. He does his duty to my satisfaction."

"Who appointed him? I never heard of his appointment till half an hour ago."

Tom coolly took the letter of the superintendent from his pocket, and exhibited it to the president.

"If that isn't all right, it isn't my fault," added the new fireman.

"That isn't worth the paper it is written on," said Tommy, his face red with wrath.

"What's the reason it isn't?" inquired Wetherstane. "I wrote it and signed it, and I am superintendent of the road."

"Did you write that?" gasped Tommy.

"I did; and I'm superintendent of the Lake Shore Railroad," answered Wetherstane, whose back was up.

"Without consulting me?"

"I didn't know that the superintendent had to go to the president every time a new fireman was wanted.

If Tom Walton isn't fireman, then I'm not superintendent."

"I won't have Tom Walton on the road," fumed Tommy, as he glanced at the fireman, who looked as good-natured as the quarter of an apple pie. "I'm president of this road."

"And I'm superintendent," retorted Wetherstane.

"Then I order you to discharge Tom Walton at once. If you appointed him, you did. Now discharge him."

Wetherstane saw that he could not very well refuse to obey this order, since his right to appoint the obnoxious fireman was not now disputed.

"I'll discharge him to-night, if you insist upon it," said he, doggedly.

"I insist upon it now. Tom Walton, you are discharged," added the president.

"I don't want to make a row, and I guess I'll be off," whispered the new fireman to me.

"You can't help yourself," I replied; and he jumped down from the foot-board.

"All aboard!" shouted the gentlemanly conductor.

I let off steam, and stepped down from the locomotive. The conductor made the signal to start; but I did not heed it; I had lost my interest in the Lightning Express.

"All right! Go ahead!" said the conductor, impatiently, when his signal was disregarded.

"Jump on your engine, and go ahead," added Tommy.

"I can't run the engine without a fireman; and I would not if I could," I replied; and I felt that I was vindicating myself.

"Do you mean to say you won't run this train?" demanded Tommy.

"That is precisely what I mean. I won't run it without Tom Walton. You discharged him on purpose to insult me."

"Where's Faxon?" asked Tommy, who seemed to be conscious, at last, that the train must go.

Faxon was in the station, and appeared to answer to his name.

"Faxon, you will run this train through," continued Tommy.

"I don't know how. I can run the dummy, but I don't know anything about running a locomotive," replied Faxon, who was among the number of those who were utterly disgusted with the tyranny of the president.

"We are five minutes behind time now," fretted the conductor, who had come forward to learn the cause of the delay.

"Here comes Major Toppleton," said half a dozen of the interested spectators.

The magnate bustled into the centre of the group, and Tommy told him I refused to run the train, and had taken that moment to spite him.

"My fireman has been discharged," I replied.

"Tom Walton!" exclaimed the major.

"Yes, sir; turned out!" laughed Tom.

"This won't do, Tommy," said the great man, pulling out his watch.

"Tom Walton can't run on this train," replied the little president, decidedly.

"Let him go this trip, till we can arrange matters," pleaded the father.

"No, sir; he shall not put foot on the engine again."

"But we are losing the trip," protested the major.

"I can't help that."

"Won't you run this trip through to oblige me?" said the magnate, taking me aside.

"I can't run it without a fireman," I replied. "I will do anything to oblige you, sir; but Tommy means to ruin me if he can."

"Start the train, and I will see that Tom Walton is with you as soon as you will need him," added the great man, in a whisper.

"I will, sir."

I jumped upon the engine, and started her, just ten minutes behind the time. I saw Major Toppleton take Tom Walton into the forward car with him, as I opened the throttle valve. The president also jumped upon the rear car, after the train started, as though he suspected the purpose of his disobedient father, and intended to defeat him. As the train went out of the station, Tom crawled over the tender, and took his place on the footboard.

"Tommy is rather rough on me," said he, with his usual good-natured smile.

"He is rough on almost everybody, and the rough-

est of all upon his own father," I replied, as I let
on more steam. "Fill up the furnace, Tom. We
are behind time, and must make up ten minutes.
We will make time as long as we are on the
engine."

In a few moments the train was flying down the
gentle slope, and, by the time we came to the up
grade beyond, Tom had steam enough to do anything
of which the engine was capable. I knew that Tommy was in one of the cars, and I wondered that he
did not stop the train, as by this time he must be
aware that his father had disobeyed and evaded his
peremptory mandate. I could hardly keep from
laughing when I thought of the magnate of Middleport, so haughty and unyielding to others, bowing
so low to his own son. It was simply ridiculous,
and very ludicrous. But I had little doubt of the
ultimate fate of Tom Walton and myself. The
world was upside down on our side of the lake,
and the great man had virtually become the little
man.

I was not quite sure that Major Toppleton could
help himself, after he had so often yielded to Tommy,

and thus encouraged him to insist upon having his own way. After abandoning his fortress even once before, I did not see how he could hold it afterwards. But all this was a question between Tommy and his father, and they must fight it out themselves. My self-respect would not any longer allow me to be the victim of his petty tyranny. Yet I have no hesitation in saying that Tommy, if his wilfulness could have been subdued, would have been one of the best fellows in the world; and the sequel of my story will justify my belief.

I had no difficulty in making up the ten minutes we had lost by the president's unseasonable demonstration, and at a quarter to ten I stopped the train at the ferry landing. I confess that my heart beat a lively tattoo against my ribs, as I saw the passengers hastening into the boat, for I dreaded a scene with Tommy and his father. I would have avoided it if I could, for I had no taste for disturbances. But neither Tommy nor his father appeared at once.

"Wolf, I don't want you to get into trouble for my sake," said Tom Walton. "I am willing to

18

take myself off, and let you live in peace with Tommy."

"Tommy don't want peace with me. Ever since our affair at the Horse Shoe, he has been down upon me," I replied. "I don't know how the major prevailed upon him to let me stay as long as I have. But he has insulted me and domineered over me in every possible manner, and I have stood just as much of it as I can. If you were not a friend of mine, Tommy would not object to you."

"Well, I don't want to stand in your way, Wolf," added Tom.

"You don't stand in my way. If you are discharged, it will be for my sake. I think we had better hang together. If I can't hold this place for you, I may be able to get you another quite as good."

"Thank you, Wolf; you have always been a good friend, and I will do just what you say. If you think it would be best for me to go, I want you to say so."

"I don't think so. My mind is made up. If you can't stay, I can't; and I shall stick to my text to the end of time," I replied, with sufficient emphasis to be understood.

The gentlemanly conductor, with the gold jewel, walked up to the engine at this moment, and interrupted our conversation.

" There's going to be the jolliest row you ever heard of," said he, chuckling as though he enjoyed the prospect.

" Where is the president? " I asked.

" He and his governor are talking over the matter in the car. The little gentleman made an awful tempest on the train, and all the passengers laughed, and enjoyed the fun. The president is going to have his own way, or drown himself in the lake," laughed the conductor.

I learned that this remark was " founded on facts," and it was evident that Tommy had not forgotten his old tricks. I stood on the engine, expecting the crash every moment; but I was ready for it.

The dummy, in charge of Lewis Holgate, stood on the track ahead of the locomotive, prepared to follow our train. Tommy and his father seemed to be having a hard time of it, for neither of them had appeared when the boat from the other side returned, and I concluded that the scene was to be deferred till a more convenient season. As the passengers were getting into the cars, I saw the major go on board of the steamer, which immediately started for the other side. A moment later Tommy approached the engine, attended by Lewis Holgate.

"Our time has come, Tom," I whispered to my companion.

"Now, Tom Walton, you will get off that engine, or the baggage masters shall pitch you off," began the president.

"I got off before when you told me," replied Tom, laughing. "I always obey orders."

"Of course you include me in the order," I added.

"I don't include you, Wolf Penniman; but you will find that you are not the president of the Lake Shore Railroad, and can't dictate to me. If you are mean enough to leave, after all we have done for you, you can do so."

I was mean enough to leave after all they had done for me, and stepped down upon the platform.

"Just as you like; but don't let me see you round this road again," continued Tommy, his face red with anger.

I walked away with Tom Walton.

CHAPTER XXIV.

THE PRESIDENT HAS A FALL.

I DO not think, after all Tommy's blustering, that he believed I would really leave the service of the Lake Shore Railroad. It was plain enough that Major Toppleton had been crowded down in the debate with his son, and had yielded the point. I supposed he had gone over to Ucayga, to avoid the unpleasant scene that was likely to ensue. In this, however, I was mistaken, for I afterwards learned that he had gone to procure the services of an engineer, for he had not much confidence in the ability of Lewis Holgate to run the locomotive.

I bought two tickets for Middleport at the office, and with Tom took a seat in one of the cars. Tommy was busy instructing Lewis in regard to his duties on the engine, of which he knew as little as any person connected with the road, and he did not follow my movements.

"Well, we are men of leisure now, Tom," I remarked, as we seated ourselves.

"I have had rather too much of that sort of thing lately, and I would rather not be a man of leisure," answered Tom, dryly.

"You will soon find something to do," I replied.

"Is Lewis Holgate going to run this train?"

"I suppose so. Tommy and he are on the best of terms; and I know that Lewis has been trying to use me up for some time, in order to get my place. I hope he is satisfied now."

"Does he understand the business?" asked Tom, curiously.

"He did very well on the dummy; but he is too careless to be relied on. I don't think he understands a locomotive. He hasn't his thoughts about him always. But I hope he will do well."

The train started, and dragged at a snail's pace for a mile. I realized from the motion that the engineer did not feel at home on the foot-board, for it was attended by frequent jerks, and by as

frequent slacking of the speed. When the conductor picked up the tickets, he told me Lewis
had with him on the foot-board a man from the
steamer, so that he could not have been embar-
rassed by having too much to do. At Grass Springs
we were ten minutes behind time; but Lewis did
better on the next stretch, which was level and
straight; but even here he was losing time, and
it was fortunate that the boat would wait at Middleport until the arrival of the train.

After we passed the Springs I saw Tommy stalk-
ing through the car, and coming towards me. I
pitied him much more than I should if he had
been defeated in his purpose, for success to him
was ruin. In spite of all he had done to vex and
annoy me, I tried to harbor no ill will against him.
He knew that the train was behind time, and that
it was still losing. I had no doubt that the fact
vexed him. It seemed to me that an opportunity
presented itself by which I could show him that
I had no ill feelings towards him. I wished still
to carry out the good principles which my mother
had taught me; and, as the little president ap-

proached my seat, I promptly decided that I would ride on the engine the rest of the way, and give Lewis such instructions as he evidently needed. I meant to do this, hoping it would make things a little pleasanter between us.

"Tommy, I suppose you see that Lewis is losing time," said I, as he halted in the aisle, and stared at me as savagely as though I had been a snake in his path.

"What are you doing here?" demanded he.

"I was going to say, if I could be of any service, I would ride on the engine with Lewis, and show him how to run it."

"I guess not," said he, shaking his head. "What are you doing here?"

"I'm going home," I replied, not comprehending what he was driving at.

"Didn't I tell you never to let me see you about this road again?" continued he, with imperial majesty, and, I may add, with lion-like ferocity.

"I believe you did; but I am going home, and the railroad is now the only conveyance up the lake."

"How dare you disobey me?" stormed he.

"I was not aware that I had disobeyed you."

"What are you on this train for, then?"

"But I paid my fare, and Tom Walton's too," I replied.

"I don't care if you did! After what has happened, I won't have you on the road."

"Even Centreporters are allowed to ride on the road by paying their fare."

"No matter if they are; you can't."

"After I get home, I won't trouble you or the road," I added, mildly.

"But you won't get home on this road," said he, seizing the connecting line which ran through all the cars to the engine, and giving it a violent twitch.

Lewis Holgate, unfortunately for me, understood this signal, and whistled to put on the brakes. The conductor was counting his tickets at the end of the car, and came forward to witness the scene. The train came to a halt.

"Now, Wolf Penniman, out with you!" said Tommy, fixing a savage gaze upon me.

"I don't wish to make any trouble, Tommy; but I have paid my fare, and I intend to ride to Middleport," I replied, as calmly as I could, though my blood was boiling with indignation at the gratuitous insults heaped upon me.

"Good, my boy! Don't budge an inch," said a respectable-looking gentleman in the seat behind me.

"Mind your own business!" snapped Tommy to the speaker.

"What, you young puppy!" said the gentleman, springing to his feet. "Don't you give me a word of impudence! If you do, I'll thrash you within an inch of your life!"

This was not exactly the kind of customer Tommy liked to deal with, for there was fight in the stranger's eye; but he was just the person whom Tommy's case required.

"Are you going to get out, Wolf Penniman, or are you going to be put out?" added the president, turning from the stranger to me.

"I'm not going to get out, and it remains to be seen whether I'm going to be put out."

"He has paid his fare," suggested the gentlemanly conductor, in a low tone.

"Give him back his money, then."

I refused to take it, and the belligerent gentleman urged me not to budge an inch.

"Put him out, conductor," said Tommy.

"If you put him out, you must put me out," suggested Tom Walton, with one of his broad, good-natured laughs.

"Put them both out!" stormed Tommy.

"I shall be prosecuted, if I do, for assault and battery."

"That's so," growled the gentleman behind me.

"I'll see you through," interposed Tommy, violently.

"This thing has gone far enough," said the stranger, rising in his seat. "This road was chartered for the accommodation of the public. These two young men have paid their fare, and have behaved themselves properly in the car. I say, for one, they shall not be put out."

"So say we all of us!" shouted several of the passengers, who were annoyed by the delay; and most of them understood the merits of the case.

"Now, conductor, start your train, and don't keep us waiting here all day," added the gentleman.

"Go ahead!" shouted some of the passengers.

"You can't go ahead till these fellows are put out," replied Tommy, who seemed to feel that he had the weather-gage in the dispute.

"Go ahead!" "Go ahead!" cried the passengers.

"Why don't you put them out, as I tell you?" said Tommy to the conductor.

"If you say so, I will, whatever happens," replied the conductor.

"I do say so!"

The proprietor of the gold jewel put his hand upon my collar; but he had hardly done so before my belligerent friend did him a similar service, and jerked him away from me. Other passengers crowded forward.

"It's an outrage! Bully for the young engineer," shouted the noisiest of the crowd.

The conductor was intimidated. He had no heart in the job he had undertaken, and he gave up with no show of fight.

"Now go ahead!" said the belligerent stranger. "We won't submit to any outrage here."

"This train won't start till those persons are put out of the car," added Tommy.

"Won't it?"

"No, it won't. I'm the president of this road," replied Tommy.

"Are you? Well, this train's going ahead," added the stranger.

To my astonishment, he seized the distinguished little functionary by the collar, and dragged him towards the door. The conductor attempted to interfere; but the passengers, among whom there were hardly a dozen Middleporters, crowded upon him, and prevented him from doing anything.

"Out with him!" "Out with him!" called the indignant passengers, not a few of whom were Centreporters.

The stout stranger landed Tommy on the ground, and then, by a dexterous movement, pitched him down the steep bank to the beach on the shore of the lake. If the president of the road was never astonished before, he was astonished then. He had

discovered that his lordly will, though it carried terror into his own family, could not accomplish much among the general public.

"Now go ahead!" said the gentleman, as he stepped into the car.

"I can't go without the president," replied the conductor.

"Then go with him!" yelled a stout fellow, who, I think, had drank more liquor than was good for him, as he seized the gentlemanly official, and hustled him after the president.

Some one pulled the string; but the train did not start. I looked out the window. I was sorry to see that Tommy appeared to be hurt, for he sat on the ground, rubbing one of his legs. The conductor went to his assistance. Lewis Holgate now appeared, and I told the stranger he was the engineer.

"Will you go ahead now?" demanded my un-compromising friend.

"What's the row here?" inquired Lewis.

He was informed; but, instead of going ahead,

he went down to the place where Tommy and
the conductor were. Several of the passengers got
out, and went forward to the engine. Half a dozen
of them beset me with entreaties to run the train
up to Middleport; but I positively refused. Indeed, I was thinking of going to the assistance
of the disabled president, though I was sure my
services would not be welcome, when the train
started. The passengers crowded in, and it was
evident that some one had taken possession of the
engine.

"Here's a pretty kettle of fish!" said Tom
Walton.

"I'm sorry for it; but I can't help it. I have
as much right to ride on this road as any one else,"
I replied.

"We are going it now," added Tom, as the
train began to leap forward at the rate of thirty
miles an hour.

"Don't you submit to any imposition, young
man. I've heard all about your case, and if you
want any help, call on me," said my belligerent
supporter.

I thanked him, and he gave me his card, which I deposited in my wallet. The new engineer understood his business, and in less than half an hour we entered the station at Middleport.

19

CHAPTER XXV.

THE PRESIDENT IN TROUBLE.

I HAD not waited to ascertain the condition of Tommy Toppleton. I had seen the stout stranger pitch him down the bank. The gentlemanly conductor had rushed down after him, to render whatever assistance he might require. Lewis Holgate had left the engine to sympathize with his powerful young friend. My occupation was gone; but I felt a certain pride and satisfaction in having stood up for my rights. I had not allowed Tommy to tread upon me this time, and I felt more like a man than I had ever felt before.

I wish to add, to some of my unreasoning young friends, that I felt an equal pride and satisfaction in the fact that I had so often submitted. I had not made haste to get into a row, and it was just as pleasant to think of what I had endured, as of the resistance I had made to oppression. If Tommy had been even tolerably reasonable, there could have been no trouble. It was a very agreeable reflection that I had not been forward in making issue with my imperious young master. If he had not been laboring to ruin me, I think I could even have borne his insults.

I was very curious to know what construction Major Toppleton would put upon my conduct. My gratitude to him made me anxious to retain his good opinion, and I had submitted to much for his sake. He certainly could not blame me for what I had done. I had merely refused to be put out of the cars after I had paid my fare. I had simply rebelled against an exhibition of petty malice, as contemptible as it was unreasonable. But, after all, it was not safe to predict what the magnate of Middleport would do when his son was involved in the affair, for the father was quite as much a victim of the young gentleman's tyranny as I was.

The stout stranger was on his way to Hitaca, and he went on board the steamer to continue his journey. Of course there was a great deal of excited talk about the incident of the day, and of the dozen Middleporters on board, those who had the courage to say anything condemned Tommy and upheld me. I thought I was safe enough; and perhaps I should have been, if exciting news had not come down from the scene of the affair.

The engineer who had taken possession of the locomotive let off the steam; and being on his way up the lake, he abandoned the machine. As there was no one to take charge of it, Wetherstane, the superintendent, asked me to run it into the engine-house, which I did. I had been duly discharged, and it was not proper for me to do anything more. I walked home with Tom Walton, and we discussed the matter as thoroughly as the occasion required.

"How do you suppose it's coming out, Wolf?" asked Tom, as good-naturedly as ever, but still anxiously.

"I haven't the least idea," I replied. "I have yielded as long as I could, and I am willing to take the consequence."

I felt that I was not likely to be a martyr as long as Colonel Wimpleton kept his offer of a place on the new steamer open to me, with the promise of a man's wages.

"If I were the major, I should rebel against Tommy a little, just to see how it would seem," laughed Tom Walton. "Don't it look strange that a great man like him — I mean the major — should be such a fool as to let his son have his own way?"

"It is strange; but I have learned that Major Toppleton is more afraid of Tommy than of all the rest of the world."

"If my mother should let me have my own way like that, I couldn't respect her. I should think the major would turn over a new leaf, and be a free man."

"He is his own master — "

"Not much!" exclaimed Tom, interrupting me; "Tommy is master here."

"Well, he has the right to obey his son, if he chooses to do so," I added. "I don't know, but I can't help thinking that this matter has come to a head now. Major Toppleton wants me to run the engine, and Tommy don't want me to do it. I hope the thing will be settled to-day."

It was settled that day.

I went home, and pretty soon my father came to his dinner. He had, of course, been my confidant in all the matters relating to my quarrel with Tommy. I told him all about the stirring events of the morning, after we sat down to dinner; and he was so interested that he neglected to touch the food before him till he had heard the whole of it.

"Have I done wrong, father?" I asked.

"Certainly not. You couldn't have done anything else. You live here, and the railroad is now the only way for you to come up the lake. You paid your fare, and they had no more right to put you off the cars than they had to throw you into the lake," he replied, warmly.

I ought to add here, that my relations with the road had been discussed every day, and often two or three times a day. My father, and my mother especially, had cautioned me not to be impulsive, and not to resist while it was decent to submit. Our obligations to Major Toppleton were acknowledged, and all of us were very anxious to keep the peace with him.

"I don't see how Major Toppleton can uphold that boy any longer," added my mother.

"I don't see how he ever could do it," said my father. "But that is his business, not mine. I don't think we make much, however, by trying to keep on the right side of these rich men by sacrificing our own self-respect. I am thankful that the major does not hold the mortgage on my house."

"I suppose he could get it, if he wanted it," suggested my mother.

"Well, it has two years to run, whoever has it; and as long as I pay the interest, we shall be safe enough," continued my father. "I am thankful we are not in such a scrape as we were on the other side of the lake."

We ate our dinner in peace, in spite of the storm which had raged without. My father was in deep thought, and it was not difficult to conjecture the subject of his meditations. Doubtless he congratulated himself most heartily that it was not in the power of either of the magnates to harass and annoy him. The major could discharge us both, and even make Middleport too warm to contain us; but the colonel was ready to receive us both with open arms. It seemed just as though I was a shuttlecock, to be batted back and forth from one side of the lake to the other at the will and pleasure of the mighty men who ruled the neighborhood.

But I had some hope that Major Toppleton would sustain me, or at least that he would not persecute our family, even if he yielded to the caprices of his son. Whatever mischief had been done, I had not done it, though I had been the indirect cause of it. I had not stopped the train; I had not put Tommy out of the car; I had not pitched him down the bank. If these things had been done on my behalf, I had no agency in them. The indignant passengers, who were detained by the whim of the little president, had been the responsible actors, and I had no doubt the stout stranger was ready to answer for his conduct. Whether he was or not, this was not my affair. I had his card in my pocket; but so far as I could ascertain, no one knew anything about him. I regarded him as a person of some consequence.

We finished our dinner, and my father was on the point of returning to the mill, when Tom Walton rushed into the kitchen, out of breath with running. His appearance indicated that some unusual event had occurred, for my friend was one of the cool sort, and not easily stirred by small matters.

"The dummy has just come in," exclaimed Tom, in the intervals between his rapid breathing.

"Well, what of it?" I inquired, not deeming this very startling intelligence.

"Tommy Toppleton's leg is broken," gasped Tom.

"Broken!" I exclaimed.

"Snapped off, like a pipe-stem, below the knee, they say."

"I am sorry for that," I added; and I almost wished it had been my leg, instead of the little tyrant's.

"His father is the maddest man that ever drew the breath of life."

"I dare say," said my father, shaking his head.

"How did it happen?" I inquired.

"Why, that stout man did it when he pitched him down the bank," answered Tom. "I'll bet it will cost that man a penny or two. That's what they say up to the station."

"I will go up and see about it," I added, taking my hat.

"You!" ejaculated Tom, with a stare of astonishment.

"Why not?"

"If you know what you are about, you will keep out of the way," suggested Tom, with significant emphasis.

"I haven't done anything that I am ashamed of," I replied. "I am not afraid to see the major, and tell him the whole story. I'm sorry for Tommy's misfortune, but it is all his own fault."

"Face the music, Wolf," said my father. "No one ever makes anything by skulking in the dark. You have a tongue, and you can explain your own conduct better than any one can do it for you."

"But they are all down upon you like a hundred

of brick, Wolf," continued Tom, who was fearful that I might be lynched in the excitement which he said prevailed in the vicinity of the major's house.

"I can't help it. When I was insulted, I did not resist nor make any row."

"But you left your train at the time it ought to have started," said Tom.

"I should not have done so if the president had not taken that time to insult me. It was not necessary for him to discharge my fireman at such a time. But no matter for all this; I am going up to Major Toppleton's house. It he chooses to kick me out, he may do so."

I could not help feeling that my chances of a fair hearing at such a time were very small, but I could not have kept away from the centre of the excitement if I had tried. I must know my fate, whatever it might be.

CHAPTER XXVI.

THE NEW STEAMER.

HOWEVER much Tommy Toppleton deserved the fate which had befallen him, I really pitied him. I am sure that not a single emotion of triumph had a place in my heart. I neither said nor thought that it served him right. I was sorry for him, and my regret was entirely unselfish. The only personal consideration that disturbed me was the reflection that I must in the future be entirely banished from the presence of Grace Toppleton. I had not the impudence, boy of sixteen as I was, to believe that I was in love with her. If such a thought had entered my head, the wide difference between her social position and mine would have driven it out.

I was deeply interested in her as a friend. She had been very kind and considerate towards me.

She had treated me with respect and regard, and did not seem to think that I was not her equal in the social scale. I never spoke to her, and never even thought of her, except with a respect bordering upon reverence. I was content to stand off at a proper distance and admire her pretty face, her graceful form, and her gentle manners. I thought she was an angel; not merely because she was beautiful in person, but because her pure heart and kind manners seemed to elevate her far above the low and selfish lives of those around her.

By the time I reached the mansion of Major Toppleton, the excitement had in a measure subsided. The bone of Tommy's leg had been set, but he was suffering severe pain. It appeared that the major had procured the services of an engineer at Ucayga, who had run the dummy up from that point, starting only half an hour behind the Lightning Express. Arriving at the place where the imperious little president had stopped our train, the magnate found the conductor and Lewis Holgate bearing Tommy towards the nearest house. He was placed in the dummy and brought home.

Of course Lewis and the conductor told their own story, and I was represented as the wickedest fellow in that part of the country. All the mischief had been done by me; and as Tommy lay writhing in agony, my sins became as mountains in the eyes of his father. Tommy was a saint then, and I was a demon.

I went to the side door of the mansion and rang the bell. The servant who opened the door bestowed upon me a look of positive horror. I inquired for Major Toppleton, and was shown into the library, where I had so often before conferred with the great man. As I was entering the room, Grace crossed the hall, and discovered me.

"O, Mr. Wolf! Why did you come here?" exclaimed she; "my father is terribly incensed against you."

"I have only done what I thought was right, Miss Grace," I replied. "I did not even know that Tommy was hurt, till a few moments ago."

"Father says you were the cause of it."

"I was not — at least, not intentionally."

"I know you were not. Whatever happens, Mr. Wolf, we shall be friends."

To my astonishment she extended her pretty, white hand, and I took it. It was her good by to me.

"I know you would not do any wrong, Mr. Wolf," she continued; "and I wish Tommy was like you."

She gently shook my hand, and left the room. Whatever her father thought, she understood the situation without any explanation. She had hardly left the room before her father came in. He looked ugly and remorseless, as he had never before been to me.

"Have you the impudence to come here, after what has happened, Wolf?" said he, with a heavy frown.

"I hope you will not consider it impudence, sir. I did not know that Tommy was hurt till a little while ago," I replied, as meekly as the occasion required. "I am very sorry indeed that anything has happened."

"Don't be a hypocrite, Wolf!"

"I am not, sir; I am truly sorry that Tommy was hurt."

"You are the cause of all this; and if you had broken his leg yourself, you would not have been more to blame."

"You have always been very kind to me, and you cannot understand the matter, or you would not say that."

"I understand it very well. I think, after all I have done for you, I had a right to expect something better from you. You insisted upon crossing and vexing Tommy."

"He was very unreasonable, and I could not submit any longer. I paid my fare in the cars, and there was no other way for me to get home."

"That's enough. You needu't attempt to explain it. Perhaps Tommy was wrong; I don't say that he was not. But it was not for you to make trouble."

"I don't think I made it, sir."

"I think you did. No more words. You have abused my good nature. I don't want to see you again. You and your father are both discharged, and the sooner you leave Middleport, the better you will suit me."

I afterwards ascertained that Tommy had insisted, even in the midst of his agony, that my father and I should be immediately discharged. Grace told me this when I met her on the lake a few weeks later in the season. She said it to defend her father, who, arbitrary as he was, had some well-defined ideas of justice.

I took my cap and left the house, after an attempt to declare that I felt no ill-will towards the major, who, however, would not permit me to finish the sentence. The catastrophe had come. The hint that the sooner our family left Middleport, the better it would suit the magnate, seemed to indicate an intention on his part to drive us out of the town. When I reached home, I found my father there. The mandate dismissing him had already been sent to him. We talked the matter over for a time; and while we both regretted Tommy's misfortune, we agreed that it would be better for both of us to work for half the wages we had been receiving, rather than be the slaves of the little magnate.

For my own part, I felt that I had borne enough

20

from Tommy. I was willing to be tried on the facts of the case, for I think no one will say that I ought to have submitted to being put out of the cars, after I had paid my fare, just to gratify the petty malice of the little tyrant. I had done my duty faithfully, even while the president of the Lake Shore Railroad had been willing to sacrifice the interest of the concern for the sake of ruining me.

In the afternoon, when it was time for the train to arrive from Ucayga, I went to the station. The Lightning Express had not appeared, and it did not come till half an hour behind time. In spite of his sufferings, Tommy still felt an interest in the outside world, and insisted that Lewis Holgate should have the locomotive. His father could not deny his request, though he knew that Lewis was incompetent. The engineer, whom the major had engaged, refused to serve as fireman under a boy, and the steamboat hand was retained in this position. The trains east and west had waited that day for the Lightning Express, or the passengers would have been compelled to lie over.

The next day, Lewis did a little better; but in the course of the week he was behind time twice; and once the conductors on the other lines refused to wait. But Tommy obstinately declined to permit his friend to be superseded by the experienced engineer who ran the dummy. Lewis declared that it was not his fault that the train was behind time; but I knew that he was lacking in judgment. He did not understand when to ease off the machine and when to crowd on the steam. He had no talent or fitness for his occupation.

I had made up my mind not to apply to Colonel Wimpleton for any situation. If he wished to employ me, and to redeem some of his large promises, he knew that I was out of a situation, and he could send for me. I did not mean to begin by cringing to him. I suppose, after the first impulses of gratitude subsided, some of the old feeling of malice towards me came back to him. It is very likely that Waddie, who had never forgiven me for deranging his plans, during the battle on the Horse Shoe, by recapturing Tommy, had some influence with his father. Whatever the reason was, I was not sent for. Father and I worked in the garden, where there was enough for both of us to do. He had money enough on hand, our joint earnings, to support the family for some months. We were both of the opinion that it was not prudent to apply to Colonel Wimpleton for situations. If he wanted us, he must come for us.

While we were thus waiting for "something to turn up," the Ucayga, the new Centreport steamer, arrived. She was certainly a magnificent boat, surpassing all the ideas I had ever formed of a floating palace. I went over to see her, and I could not but realize that she would be a formidable rival of the Lightning Express, even if she did require half an hour longer to make the trip. On her passage down the lake, she had made sixteen miles an hour without pressing; but as half her freight and passengers depended upon Ruoara, she was to be allowed an hour and three quarters for the trip, against an hour and a quarter required to make the passage by the Lake Shore Railroad.

Flaming posters about the streets of Centreport announced that the Ucayga would leave at quarter past eight, and connect with the trains east and west at the foot of the lake. It all looked very pretty, but the battle was yet to be fought. The competition was for through-passengers. When the boats from Hitaca reached Centreport twice each day, the question with travellers was to be, whether they would go to Ucayga by the new steamer or by the railroad. The boats from up the lake usually arrived at quarter past eight and quarter past two, allowing fifteen minutes at Centreport, and fifteen more to land their passengers at Middleport. If the Ucayga could get off on time, she was safe enough on her connections. It was a question of minutes and seconds on which the success of the steamboat enterprise depended. But of the hard-fought battle which ensued, I shall speak in another story — "On Time."

Everybody in Centreport and Middleport was excited over the impending contest, for it was still a battle between the two sides of the lake. Major Toppleton professed to be entirely confident of the result, and mysteriously hinted at resources for winning the race which had not yet been developed.

The Ucayga made her first trip crowded with passengers, while the Lightning Express train was com-
paratively deserted. Still the major was confident,
declaring that "a new broom sweeps clean," but
the passengers would soon return to the railroad,
especially during the approaching winter, when the
steamer was liable to be troubled with ice in the
lower part of the lake.

But a shadow soon came over the dream of
Colonel Wimpleton, who boasted grandiloquently
over his success. The up-lake boats began to be
regularly ten minutes late; and one day, in spite
of all the crowding done on board of the Ucayga,
she missed her connections. Then she did it again,
and again, and people would not trust her. Steamer stock went down. As Major Toppleton's hopes
rose, Colonel Wimpleton's fell. It was plain enough
now that the major required the Hitaca boats to be
ten minutes late. The colonel swore terribly when
he realized the nature of the trick.

As my connection with the Lightning Express
had ceased, it would not be proper for me to remain any longer under that flag; and I must take

leave of the Lake Shore Railroad for the present, to forage in a new field.

About the time the Ucayga arrived at Centreport, Tommy Toppleton was able to leave the house on crutches. The only word the major had spoken to me since our interview in his mansion, was to tell me that I had lamed his son for life. I did not believe this, and it was a great satisfaction for me to hear the doctor say that Tommy's leg would be as good as ever in a few weeks. I hoped his sufferings would do him good, and do something to modify his arbitrary character.

I need hardly say that the rival Academies were still rivals. Neither was satisfied with the result of the battles on the Horse Shoe, and each was thirsting for an opportunity to overwhelm the other. I could not justify myself for giving the details of this miserable warfare, if it were not for contrasting it with the glorious peace and fraternity which grew out of it.

Tommy was, perhaps, as unpopular as ever; but his misfortune, if it did not excite the sympathy of the Toppletonians, prevented them from manifesting their feelings in a mutiny, as they intended, at my discharge. I am happy to say that I stood first rate with the students on the Middleport side, when Tommy and his father had done their worst; but the mutiny came at last, when Tommy's tyranny could be no longer endured. I was satisfied. I shall always remember with pleasure most of my experience on the Lake Shore Railroad, and especially on the LIGHTNING EXPRESS.

www.ingramcontent.com/pod-product-compliance
Lightning Source LLC
Chambersburg PA
CBHW060516030726

47498CB00004B/963